To The Moon, Alice!

Book 1 - Me and the Maniac in Outer Space

Robert Alexander Swanson

Prevail Press

Prevail Press

Contents

Chapter 1

Bullies

MY YOUTH PASTOR WAS trying to describe Hell yesterday. It didn't take. We were 13-year-olds, most of us skinny, brainy and short. He was wasting his time because we already knew.

I attended Baltoc Middle School. It was 8th grade P.E. and class was over. P.E. is like purgatory, if I were Catholic, which I'm not, in that it's suffering and evil, but nowhere near as bad as Hell itself. Hell is the boy's locker room.

The locker room looked hungry, and it smelled like it ate only corn chips. Kentucky is warm in May, but I shivered in my too-large shorts anyway. Best to get it over with. I bee-lined for my locker, a modern-day torture device because you had to put your hands into it to retrieve your clothes, meaning any larger 9th grader—and they were all larger—could slam the clattering metal door on your wrist or fingers if your guard wasn't up or you weren't fast enough.

At my size, my guard was always up and my reflexes were honed to top speed, and still I almost lost my fingers. Jason Pruit, hulking, dumb and hairy, slammed my locker door, making everyone look at me in the one place you absolutely want to be invisible.

"You're supposed to take a shower, dimwit!" Pruit grated, upset that he hadn't crushed my hand.

No way. First, I didn't work hard enough in P.E. to sweat and second, even if I did, there was no way I was entering the ninth ring of Hell that was the group shower bay. Small, skinny kids break easily on all those hard tile and metal surfaces: "He slipped, Coach!" Meanwhile, my life's blood swirls down the drain.

I didn't say any of that to Pruit, though. Besides it being uber-creepy that he'd care, I wasn't going to give him a better excuse to kill me than just the mumbling I offered instead.

"You know what we do with dirty kids, right?" he leered, shaking a can of shaving cream. Yes, Pruit shaved, and he loved to let everyone know it. Other kids gathered around to watch, the small ones with wide and grateful eyes that it wasn't them.

TO THE MOON, ALICE!

Last week, Pruit had shoved me into the locker. It was quite spacious, however, so I really didn't mind. As violence goes, that was pretty easy. This, though, was solid cruelty. After getting lathered, the shower would be required, probably by that time under the watchful eyes of a coach who loves Pruit and somehow will believe I'd dowsed myself with shaving cream. Coach wasn't much of an improvement over Pruit. Oh, he wouldn't hit me or slam me around, he'd just lecture me on standing up like a man, my 75 pounds against Pruit's 175 pounds. He's a P.E. coach, not a math teacher. I'd have to be crazy to take on Jason Pruit.

Fortunately, my best friend was crazy.

Pruit suddenly lurched, dropping the can, which squirted shaving cream all over Pruit's shoes. Spinning to kill whoever had kidney-punched him, Pruit slipped and crashed into the lockers, drawing laughter even from the little kids. Huffing and puffing like the Big Bad Wolf, Pruit carefully swiveled to confront his attacker. And then he sagged.

"Not you, you little maniac," Pruit said with a sigh of exasperation.

Jack Taylor, AKA The Maniac and my best friend, looked up at Pruit with a cocky grin. The Maniac wasn't any bigger or heavier than me. His hair was dirty blond, and no one knew if it was actual dirt. Since his clothes were always dirty, maybe his hair was too. It tended to drape over his eyes, which added to the illusion that he was crazy. And by every small kid's definition, Jack was.

Just like the coach always told me, Jack stood up to everyone, no matter how big. Oddly, the coach didn't like Jack much, and neither did anyone but us small kids, and most of them were terrified of Jack.

Jack was a scrapper. He enjoyed fighting, if you could call it that. If Pruit engaged—which he wouldn't, it was already obvious—Jack would take any punishment Pruit could dish out and for every punch Pruit would land, Jack would land or bite four. If Jack's nose got bloody, he'd smear it all over his opponent. He'd bite, kick, pull hair, scream, tear clothes... he might not win the fight, but it would be so costly to the winner it just wasn't worth it. Worse, even pounded and bloody, Jack would never lose that grin. You could abuse his body, but you'd never touch his spirit.

Did I mention we were best friends?

As Pruit tried to swagger away without looking weak, Jack grinned that maniacal grin and said, "To the moon, Alice!" and punched me hard on the shoulder. That's Jack.

The Maniac was from a poor, broken family. It was just him and his dad now, less said about that, the better. They couldn't afford cable, so the only TV they had was a bunch of VHS tapes of an old black-and-white show called "The Honeymooners" starring someone called Jackie Gleason. My Jack idolized him and his favorite phrase was "To the moon, Alice!"

"Thanks, Jack," I said, rubbing my shoulder.

"Sure thing, Hud," Jack said. My real name is Hudson Cook, but there's just no good abbreviation for my name. "Hud" sounds like a guy similar to Pruit only dumber.

"Need any help with your homework?" I asked.

Jack grinned. "Nope!"

"Did you do your homework?"

"Nope!"

This was part of our ritual. He'd save my bacon, I'd offer to do his homework, he'd say no. It was his way of saying we were friends and he'd save me for nothing.

We were unlikely friends. Jack is actually a lot smarter than he pretends to be, and I'm a lot smarter than I appear to be, which is smart because I wear glasses and have an inquisitive expression that I can't seem to change.

Also, I'm a Christian and Jack isn't, and my family is pretty well-off since both my parents are IT specialists, which means they work with computers. Mom works from home so she can take care of my new baby sister,

Elatys, which means "Surprise" in Finnish, sort of, on account of Ela being a surprise for all of us.

I think Mom must have wanted a lot of kids because she treats Jack like he was my brother. All my teachers said he's a bad influence since I was clearly a bright boy who didn't get the grades I should be getting. That's true, but it's because it bore me out of my mind in every class except P.E. where I was scared out of my mind instead.

I got dressed as quick as I could while Jack, a few lockers down, took his time. He was the only untouchable kid in school. I guess when you haven't got anything to lose, bravery is easy. Me, I should be brave because my dad says we're distantly related to Admiral Cook, the great explorer. I guess he was too distant, because I was scared all the time. Dad says that will go away when I'm out of school or if I beef up over the next few years and that, meanwhile, I could take strength from Jesus. I wish. Jesus is cool. He's every bit the explorer as great-great-uncle Cook, braving the wilds of Earth instead of staying safe in Eternity. He didn't get such a good deal down here, though, but he was never afraid. I wish I could be like that.

"You really didn't do your homework?" I said.

"Naw, it's History. I'll just pretend to read my report and make it up as I go along."

"Cool." And it was. Jack would spin an incredible story and go on and on until Miss Hardy stopped him, which took a long time because she enjoyed it as much as we did. Miss Hardy told Jack he had a wonderful future ahead of him but it would help if he did his homework.

Miss Hardy was good like that. All the other teachers expected Jack to fail miserably in life. Didn't matter to Jack, he had other plans.

For as long as I've known Jack, his overriding goal was to discover new caves. We live a few towns over from Mammoth Caves, part of a network of vast underground caverns that stretched out under the countryside. New caves were found regularly and Jack and I spend most of our free time tramping through the woods looking for caves. We've found several, all carefully marked on a map of Jack's own devising. They hadn't gone very far, but it was enough to keep us hunting.

***

The final bell finally rang and kids poured out of the school like rats off a sinking ship. History had gone well, I fell asleep in English, floundered in Spanish and pounded my head on the desk during Pre-Algebra. The only fun class was Home Ec. where we made root beer-flavored cake, but I couldn't exactly admit that to anyone.

It wasn't that learning was bad, it's just the turtle-slow teaching that killed me; that and the dumb questions kids asked (there are too dumb questions!). I was confident that the entire school day could be crammed into an hour and even then, only if P.E. took 15 minutes.

Jack simply doodled through every class except the dreaded P.E. and math class. Jack loved numbers. I wasn't altogether certain he could read, but numbers could dance a jig for him. His grades didn't reflect it, though. Ask Jack a question out loud and he'd have the answer. Make him read the question and forget it.

He was also gifted in strategy and loaded with compassion. Whenever Jack faced down an upper-classmen, chances were good a gang of bullies would be waiting at the curb for us after school. Jack, of course, would love nothing better than wading into them, but for my sake, he invented ways to escape them. Sometimes it meant leaving school from the back and going home through the woods, other times we walked right past them as we escorted Miss Hardy to the Administration Building across the street.

This was Monday, though, so our escape included four wheels and that gym locker corn-chip smell. The first day of the school week was laundry day. I guess they wanted the locker room towels to get nicely ripe over the weekend.

A big cargo van pulled up to the loading bay at precisely 3 o'clock. Mackie Windsor was the driver and our friend.

"Hey, Mackie!" Jack howled.

"My man, the Maniac!" Mackie crowed back. "Who'd you tick off this time?"

"Pruit," I said.

"Bummer, dude. His big brother beat me up every other week when I went here."

We knew this, of course, since he mentioned it every time we saw him. Mackie was a geek like us, working to save up money to go to college. A school you had to pay for; I couldn't even imagine.

"Help me with the bags, huh?" Mackie said.

We complied, walking the last two bags into the van and sitting on them. Mackie smiled and closed the doors. As we pulled out of the school parking lot, we heard Mackie holler, "Yo, man, say hello to your brother for me!" and imagined him flashing the peace sign at Pruit and his gang.

"How adventurous are you guys today?" Mackie called out.

"Very!" Jack shouted, ignoring my shaking head. I sighed. Mackie stopped at the next turn, well within sight of Pruit's posse. Jack popped the doors and we scrambled out and slammed them shut.

"Later, dudes!" Mackie waived and honked the horn, drawing the eyes of Pruit and the bruisers.

Jack flashed his version of the peace sign at them with one less finger than Mackie's and we took off running. Naturally, they took off after us.

We took the turn and saw unbroken road ahead of us and chain-link fence twice as high as we were with razor-wire on top protecting the woods from us on either side of the street. This was way too much like P.E. to me. We were out of sight of our tormentors for as long as it would take them to make that turn themselves. If we were caught on the road when they did, it wouldn't take them long to run us down. All we had to do was make it to the third post of the imposing fence.

"Don't look back!" Jack yelled. Too late, I already had. The third post was coming up; how fast were the bruisers today? No one was behind us. We hit the fence at full throttle, sliding through the hidden seam. I plunged down the embankment and into the trees while Jack spun and secured the fence so the seam that was unknown to anyone but us would stay hidden.

Jack melted into the trees and showed up beside me with a finger to his lips. I was breathing heavily and there was nothing I could do about it, but I tried.

Moments later, feet pounded by on the street above us but quickly trailed off as they slowed down, realizing we were gone. "No way!" one of the boys shouted.

"Yeah, no way. Nobody's that fast." Pruit's voice.

"No way they climbed that fence, either," said the first boy.

That was worrisome. They were actually applying logic.

"There must be a break in the fence," Pruit said. I didn't think he had it in him. "Find it!"

Jack suddenly cried out, "Don't touch it! It's electrified!"

"Whoa!" said the first voice.

We heard a smack and then, "They went through it, idiot, it isn't hot!"

Jack smirked and beckoned me further into the woods. "They'll find the seam!" I whispered.

"Doesn't mean they'll find us," Jack replied.

Jack and I slipped through the trees, trying to stay quiet as they pounded the fence looking for give. We were maybe 30 feet into the woods when they found it. One of them fell down the embankment, making a lot of noise. The startled yelp sounded different from the other two voices, which meant all three of the bullies had come after us.

Jack moved quietly through the woods. The landscape around here was composed of low hills and valleys with overgrown trees and brush shrouding drop-offs and, as it turned out, a cave. Jack hadn't told me about this one. He simply parted the brush, climbed through, and disappeared. I gingerly followed and found myself in a low-ceilinged cave. With no candles or flashlights, I couldn't tell how deep it went in. Shallow caves can sometimes be the home of animals, or it could be one that goes on for miles.

Great crashing sounded through the woods as our would-be killers searched frantically for us. While the cave had been completely invisible from outside, we could still see into the trees as afternoon light slanted into the woods. Pruit staggered into sight, fighting the underbrush. When he pitched head-long and landed on his face, I slapped a hand over Jack's mouth and just barely smothered his laughter. Pruit's head came up, brambles in his hair as if he'd heard either the slap or the giggle. He looked around silently as another tormentor broke into the valley. Pruit shushed him and they both remained still.

"Guys?" quavered the third from some distance off. "Hey, guys?"

"Quiet!" yelled Pruit, and they were.

Jack started to tap his foot, which was never a good sign. He was getting bored.

Pruit picked up some pebbles and began tossing them into bushes, hoping to hit us. He wasn't being as stupid as I'd prefer.

Jack was no longer at my side. Looking around, I saw him scrambling for pebbles of his own. I shook my head at him. He smiled at me. Sneaking closer to the cave opening, he peered through the masking brush and waited. When Pruit and his buddy weren't looking our way, he zinged a rock up the hill beyond them. Their heads snapped to the sound.

"Was that you, Tommy?" Pruit called. Nothing. "Tommy?"

Suddenly, Tommy came stumbling over the hill they were staring at. He took a misstep and tumbled into a pricker bush, yelling bloody murder. Those things had long thorns and Tommy tried to rise in the middle of it, sinking back down as the thorns cut into him. I wasn't sure, but I think he was crying.

Pruit looked on with disgust.

"Get me out of here, Pruit!"

Pruit looked around once more and shook his head. "Get yourself out, moron." He grabbed his friend, who resisted for a moment, then allowed himself to be pulled after Pruit.

"You're leaving? Hey, come on, guys! I need help! Guys! It's going to get dark soon!" He kept calling after his friends but it became clear they were long gone. Tommy sat down and bawled.

Jack moved toward the mouth of the cave, and I stopped him. "It could be a trick!" I whispered. Jack shook me off and stepped through the brush. I grabbed some rocks and followed him. Jack strode toward Tommy while I looked around frantically.

"Some friends, huh, Tommy?" Jack said.

Tommy fisted tears from his eyes. "Help me out, would you?" he said.

"You were going to beat us up," I said.

"No, I wasn't. I was just gonna watch."

"Oh, yeah, that's better," I said and looked around for Jack. He was hunting around the ground, couldn't find what he was looking for, and headed over the hill.

"Don't leave me!" cried Tommy.

"He's not," I said. "That isn't Jack's way."

Soon, Jack came back with two long, heavy branches. We stripped it free of leaves and smaller branches, turning them into poles. He took one, and I took the other. We shoved them into the center of the prickly bush above Tommy's head and out the other side.

"Don't move and maybe cover your head." Jack said. Tommy was pretty scratched up and any movement made it worse.

We held onto our poles and walked away from each other, trying to spread the bush apart. It was slow going, as the prickly branches were wrapped around each other. We worked the poles with Tommy occasionally crying out as a branch whacked him. Finally, a path through the bush emerged. Ten minutes later, Tommy was free.

We started plunking thorns off of him, Tommy yelped with each one. When we cleared most of them away, Jack pointed him back toward the road.

"Aren't you guys coming?" Tommy asked.

"Nope," Jack said.

"Oh. Okay, then. Thanks, I guess," Tommy said.

"No more hunting kids," I said.

"Just one more. I'm gonna get my brother and we're gonna beat the snot outta Pruit!"

"Take pictures," I said.

"What happened to 'turn the other cheek?'" Jack said.

Jack had a habit of turning Christianity back on me. I considered. "Hey, Tommy, let me know after you do it and I'll pray for Pruit," I said and turned to Jack. "Better?"

"If you say so," Jack said, and he tromped off deeper into the woods. I followed him, knowing I'd let down God again.

"Cool cave," I said.

"Yeah," Jack said.

Two sets of woods and three crossed roads later, we were at my house.

"You comin' in?" I said.

"Naw," Jack said, but I knew he wanted to.

"Fresh-baked cookies," I said. "And I'm sure Mom held out some dough for you."

Jack doesn't like baked cookies, but he loves cookie dough. He gave up without much of a fight.

Trooping in, sure enough, a heavenly smell filled the house. In the kitchen, Mom had Ela strapped into her highchair and was spooning orange mush into her mouth. Cookies cooled on a rack and a bowl of cookie dough was right beside it.

Mom put down the spoon and scooped us both into a big hug. "My little men home from school!"

"Mom!" I said. Jack just beamed. Ela gurgled. Jack wiggled his fingers at her.

"Wash your hands and dig in," Mom said, returning to the baby.

We complied, leaving our wrists encrusted with dirt.

"I really shouldn't let you eat dough, Jack," she said, like always. "I scooped that bit out before I added the eggs—you shouldn't eat raw eggs, you know—but I still think it's better to eat the cooked ones."

Jack wrinkled his nose and scooped a finger-full of dough.

"Mom," I said, "there's nothing healthy about cookies, whether they're cooked or not."

"Chocolate's a food group, dear," she said.

"Only in this house," I said.

"Aren't you fortunate," she said, and I knew I was. "Staying for dinner, Jack?" Mom asked.

"No, Ma'am, gotta make something for my dad."

"When are you going to bring that man over, Jack? It's been way too long. We'd love to have you both for dinner," Mom said.

"Next time he's sober, Mrs. Cook, I promise."

Mom wrapped Jack in another hug. She's just like that, I guess.

CHAPTER 2

Classes and Caving

S CHOOL WAS ONLY MILDLY torturous for the rest of the week. Pruit was lying low with a black-eye while Tommy was playing up the story of his many scratches. He hadn't gotten pictures, but I borrowed a friend's phone and snapped one when Pruit wasn't looking and e-mailed it to myself. As uber-geeky as my parents were, they hadn't given me a cell-phone yet. Maybe for my birthday in a couple of months.

Middle School is a weird place. In Grade School, everything made sense. Then, a couple of grades later, nothing does. Before, girls were to be ignored or chased. Now they were vaguely uncomfortable to be around and really uncomfortable not to be around.

"What is it with girls?" Jack had asked. He was always a little slow when reality shifts.

"What do you mean?" I said. I knew what he meant, of course, but had no answers. We were standing in the school's courtyard during lunch with kids milling around, texting and gabbing. Well, I was standing and Jack was fidgeting. Standing still was not his strength.

"Girls used to be like guys who you weren't allowed to hit," he said.

"And now?"

We watched a girl go by in pink jeans and a frilly shirt.

"Now I don't want to hit them," he said. "And yet, I do want to. What is that?"

"That's just unfair, that's what it is." We watched a few more girls and still couldn't figure it out.

Truthfully, I think about that question every day in Spanish class. When I'd talked to my dad about which second language I should take, he'd summed it up like this: "German is the easiest, Spanish is the most useful, and French will help you pick up babes." At the time, I'd opted for Espanola because German would be boring and French would be gross. Now it was too late to switch.

Jack stuck out his tongue at another girl walking by, this one in shorts and a sweater (who wears sweaters in May?). She just sniffed and lifted her nose in the air.

Jack sighed. "See? She should have stuck her tongue out and started running. Why don't they run anymore, Hud?"

English was our last class on Friday, and the clock was doing a great impression of a snail.

"Hudson," my teacher said, interrupting her lesson, "you're going to bruise your forehead if you keep doing that."

Leaving my head on the desk, I responded, "Why do we have to take English if it's our mother tongue?"

"I'm failing Spanish," Juan, our Mexican immigrant, said.

"How weird is that?" Jack said.

"Not as weird as me acing English," Juan replied.

Everyone else got into the discussion, effectively ending class for the day. Even the teacher looked relieved.

The walk home was hot and wonderful. Jack was carrying his t-shirt in his hand, exposing his white-white skin to the sun. I kept mine on because I didn't burn, I freckled and who wants freckles on their chest? In my case, there'd only be room for one. I resolved to start working out, but knew it was a lie even as I thought it.

"What do you want to do this weekend?" I said.

Jack appeared to think about. "How 'bout we look for caves?" He always said that.

"Sounds good to me," I said, like always.

Jack didn't have the attention span for video games and I'd already beaten all the ones I had. I was too small for the neighborhood scrub football game and Jack was too vicious. That left exploring.

"Wanna start now?" I said.

Jack kicked at a rock on the sidewalk. "Naw, I gotta go get my dad."

"Want me to come along?"

"Your parents wouldn't like that."

"My parents love you more than they love me."

Jack grinned. "Who wouldn't?" and took off running. If it weren't for Jack, I wouldn't get any exercise at all. He ran like a spaz, arms and legs flailing, so I had a chance of catching him.

Taking a left down the hill instead of straight to my house, we picked up speed on the downslope. Fortunately, I wasn't really trying to catch him and he stopped when I shifted to walking.

Up ahead, the road forked. Town was to the left and Old Town was to the right. Old Town wasn't really a town at all. It had sprung up when bars were zoned out of the city. Now that those zoning laws were gone, only the worst places were in Old Town. We took the right fork. I'd gone with Jack many times before, but it still skeeved me out. Jack was right. My parents would freak if they knew I was here.

The best of the worst places were in the center of Old Town. Jack's dad, Big Jack, was in the worst of the worst on the outside of Old Town, so fortunately, we didn't have to pass any other places.

If this tavern ever had a sign with its name on it, it didn't anymore. It was a sprawling shack with more tar paper showing than siding. Big Jack's old truck was in the gravel lot. We pushed through a squeaky door and the few people inside flinched at the noise.

Big Jack sat in a torn booth behind a broken pool table with no felt. His usual place on Fridays. His eyes were watery and unfocused. He looked at Jack without immediate recognition.

The bar was a long piece of plywood set up on two metal barrel things. The bartender was a portly Asian person, probably a man, but it was hard to tell in the low light and folds of fat. He/she never spoke, but keys materialized on the plywood as we passed by. Jack snatched them up without looking.

"Time to go home, Dad."

"'S'not dark yet," Big Jack said.

I looked around. The windows were so dirty the only light came from a discarded chandelier that seemed out of place here. How did he know the sun was still up?

"Put on your sunglasses, Dad. Bartender won't draw any more."

"Still have money," Big Jack slurred.

"Show me," Jack said.

Big Jack searched the tabletop, then his pockets, and dragged out what he found there. A crumpled napkin, a few lottery tickets, nothing else.

"Where're my keys?" Big Jack rumbled.

"I got 'em, Dad."

"Got any money?"

The smell in here was making me ill. "Come on, Big Jack, let's go," I said.

He seemed to see me for the first time. "Yer not old 'nough to be in here, boy."

"Jack's here, sir," I said. I was older than Jack.

"'e's a good boy."

"Yes, sir."

There was a scuffling from under the table as Big Jack found his feet. Big Jack is big, so the table tipped as he tried to get up. Jack and I leaned on the other side. "Slide around first, Dad."

He shuffled and dragged himself to the edge and lumbered up, catching himself on the booth back and Jack's shoulder. Jack somehow stood up to the weight. I scurried around and got under Big Jack's other arm and headed to the door.

"Don' forget to get my change," Big Jacked weaved.

"Sure thing, Dad," Jack said, ignoring the bartender's contemptuous gaze.

Big Jack thrust through the door and reeled back, throwing an arm over his eyes. "W're my glasses."

"Probably in the truck, Dad."

"Go fetch 'em."

"Quicker to take you to 'em, Dad, just close your eyes and we'll guide you."

I blinked my eyes in the sunlight, too. Once we got to the truck, we maneuvered Big Jack to the back. Jack reached over and opened the tailgate catch. There was a mattress in the bed of the truck. A bed in the bed, I thought, and bit my lip to keep from laughing what was no doubt a hysterical laugh.

Jack leaned his dad back onto the gate and helped him scoot up and sprawl on the mattress. Jack deftly pulled some webbing over Big Jack and secured it to cleats in the rusting sides. Big Jack was already asleep, and the webbing was like a rubber blanket over him. He probably wouldn't wake up, but he had once before and tumbled out of the truck onto the road. Since then, the webbing was a must.

TO THE MOON, ALICE!

We climbed into the cab and were hit by the rank smell of beer and something else. Big Jack picked up day work when he could. Used to be construction, but as he got worse, mucking stalls and raking paddocks was about all he could do. I'd asked Jack to come live with us, but he'd said somebody had to take care of his dad.

Big Jack could have sat in the bar until dark, but once evening came around, police would begin cruising the streets and we wouldn't be able to do what we're doing now. Jack pulled an old phone book out of the passenger's foot well and sat on it, then pulled the seat as far forward as he could. It was a big truck, though, so he could barely see over the steering wheel and touch the pedals, so he stood as much as he sat.

Starting the engine, he looked around as best he could and, seeing no police, he carefully pulled out onto the street. We made it the three miles home, just beyond the Old Town "city" limits, without any problems. Once Jack grew another foot, he'd be a terrific driver.

We got out and Jack opened the gate, unhooked the webbing and looked at the sky. No clouds, so he left his father where he was. He could find his own way into the house once he woke up.

Jack lived down a dirt road in a four-room house where one of them was a bathroom that mostly worked. There

25

was a pond out back beyond the weeds and a barn of sorts with mildewed hay and no animals. I was never clear if they actually owned the house and never asked.

When I first met Jack, we were three years old and our mothers met at the neighborhood playground. Big Jack had been a normal man then, building homes and doing good. They lived four houses down from us. Then Jack's mom had died from some kind of cancer that took as much life as it could before the disease drank down the rest of it.

Me and Jack had been in kindergarten then, or at least I was. Jack didn't come much. He would have been left behind, but his mom had kept schooling him even when she was really sick. She'd passed at the beginning of summer vacation. By fourth grade, the Jacks moved out of our neighborhood and into this place and Big Jack got worse every year since.

"C'mon, I'll walk you home."

"I'm not a girl. I can walk by myself."

"Think your mom has some cookie dough left?"

What he really meant was did my mom have any hugs left, and I knew she did so we walked to my home together.

Jack is an early riser on the weekends and I am not, so it's common for me to wake up and go to breakfast with Jack already finishing up, talking with my mom.

"...you won't go too far?" my Mom was saying as I wandered in.

Jack had his map spread out on the table, carefully away from the omelet Mom had made him. We always ate better when Jack dropped by because Mom was worried it was the only meal he'd be getting that day, even though I knew Jack was actually really good at scrounging what he needed.

"No, ma'am. See here? No matter where we go, we've always got a main road within 20 minutes of walking distance and I always have my compass." His feet tapped frantically under the table. He was always at his stillest when Mom was around.

What he didn't tell her was that the other side of the map had the real woods we'd been searching. Jack didn't consider it a lie because he knew we'd never get lost. Even without a compass, Jack could find his way back from anywhere.

After my own eggs and toast, we were off with a rucksack of flashlights, candles, matches, rope, bug spray and an emergency GPS transponder, just in case. We had to walk to the woods because Jack didn't have a bike. We'd bought him several, but they always went missing, which meant Big Jack probably sold them when we were at school. That was okay with me, though, because big-time explorers never used bikes.

We trooped by several horse paddocks, all of them with girls riding the horses. What was it with girls and horses? We watched closely as we went by in case the answer would spring up from the dirt.

Finally, we got to the woods we wanted to search. We'd already fished out the closer woods. This one was really big and if I'd been with anyone but Jack, I'd be a little afraid to go in there. This one went on for miles and had a history of long-ago strange lights and ghostly tales. Some say kids went in there and got lost, never to return.

The forests of Kentucky are filled with legends centered on Indians and slave ghosts screaming in the night. It draws a lot of tourists, but Dad took all the mystery out of it when told me it was just foxes, rabbits and peacocks raising a ruckus. They sound just like humans when they're mad. It's still a pretty good deal for visitors, though, because the woods around here are spectacular and varied. Some have skinny trees and sparse grounds easy for hiking. Others, like this one, were shaggy, uneven and overgrown. They looked like something out of pre-history. Deadfalls overgrown with moss, mounds that could be hills of earth or just piles of brush and giant trees leaning with age hid all sorts of, we hoped, caves.

TO THE MOON, ALICE!

I'm pretty sure Mom would strangle us if she knew we were here. Breaking a leg would be easy with all the rotting wood giving way beneath you, but this is where being light and skinny worked for us. We could scramble over things that could be deadly to bigger people.

I loved combing through woods with Jack. All the things weighing him down and all the defense he puts up to keep other kids from making fun of him dropped away when we were out here. Intensity gripped Jack, that contrasted sharply with his usual devil-may-care attitude. I was out here for fun, but Jack was out here to work!

We would find a high rise in the forest and Jack would scan the area, particularly the depressions and valleys, to "read" the land. If no hills were handy, Jack would shinny up a tree. As I've said, we've found many caves like this over the years. The older we got, the more frantic Jack became to find the Big One, a cave that reached deep and wide below us.

It was weird to know that the ground beneath us could very well be hollow. Layers of limestone get eaten away over the centuries while the sandstone on top wears away much slower. The sandstone is hard and stable, allowing just the occasional entrance to the vast, meandering chambers beneath it, but dirt or underbrush often covered those entrances.

We explored dozens of likely places, poking sticks or throwing rocks to penetrate the overgrowth. After several hours, we gave up long enough to eat sandwiches and drink two juice boxes each.

"We need to go further in," Jack said.

"Maybe there aren't any caves, Jack."

"There are, just further in."

"Jack, this was further in before they built the roads out there. There's no difference between 'in there' and 'out here.'"

Jack looked at me like I'd betrayed him. He crumpled the wax paper and flattened his juice boxes and shoved them into the front pouch of the rucksack.

"I'll just go on without you, then," he said and stalked away.

Like I had any choice but to follow him. I'd never find my way out on my own. I stowed my garbage and hefted the bag. If he'd really thought I'd go home, he would have kept the bag.

I made it to the top of the hill just as he lost his footing on the steep down-slope and slid feet first into the moss-covered foothill. I was amused until Jack suddenly disappeared as if he'd fallen through the earth!

"Yes!" echoed a cry from where I'd last seen Jack. How about that? He had fallen through the earth. "Hey! Toss me a flashlight and get down here!"

Friends again, I gingerly made my way to the lip of the drop-off hole in the moss. "Let me tie off a rope and get down there!"

"No need," echoed his voice. "There's another entrance down the way!"

I made the mistake of peering over and found myself slipping. No amount of back-pedaling helped, so I gave up and dropped. "Bombs away!" I called, hoping I wouldn't break my neck.

Fortunately, Jack broke my fall.

After we gathered ourselves up and Jack punched my arm for falling on him, we broke out the flashlights.

Our warren hole above us and our own beams showed the cave branched out in two directions. One ran a short way to another, larger, ground-level entrance, just as Jack had said. The other stretched beyond our flashlight's reach.

Jack practically jumped up and down. "This is it! This is the Big One!"

"Not necessarily," I said, forever the wet blanket.

"Let's go find out!"

"Smell any gas?" I said. Too long in a methane-soaked cave and we'd be sleeping here forever.

"Light a candle and find out," Jack said.

Right, and blow ourselves up. I sniffed at the air instead. Musty and loamy smelling, but not gassy, I decided.

Caves were formed by running water, which took the easiest path it could, meaning if there were varying degrees of hardness in the limestone, the cave might have really cool characteristics. This one had the sandstone ceiling just out of reach above us. Thousands of years ago, there were two layers of limestone, the one on top so soft that it wore away and was now gone. The second layer was waist high from the floor with rounded channels cut through it. At its closest points, we could barely touch either side with outstretched fingertips and at its widest, it was maybe eight feet.

The further we went in, though, the narrower it got, and then something strange happened. Jack yelped. He'd been running his fingers along the rounded edge and suddenly it was no longer rounded.

We played our flashlight beams on the edges of both sides. While they weren't exactly sharp, they had definitely been cut, artificially keeping the channel at least five feet wide. Jack's yelp had been in surprise, not pain, fortunately. Aiming upward, we saw the ceiling was sloping down closer to our heads.

"If someone was here to cut it, why isn't the cave on any maps?"

"Maybe it is," I said. "Maybe it's too small to be a big deal."

Jack aimed his light forward. While the channel we were walking in ended up ahead, the cave itself stretched a long way beyond his flashlight beam, at least for forty more feet. "It's plenty big. If we hop out of the channel and walk up here," he said, patting the shelf in which our channel had been cut, "I bet it goes all the way to the edge of the woods and maybe beyond. Come on!" He hoisted himself up onto the shelf.

"Why would someone cut this channel wider?" I said, not following him.

"Huh?" Jack said.

"You're right, you can always jump up there and keep going. Why go to the trouble of cutting the limestone?"

"It's easy to cut."

"But why?"

We both played our beams to the end of our channel. It stopped at a rock wall twenty feet away. Jack shrugged, remained on the shelf, and walked toward the wall. I did the same, staying in the channel.

Nothing remarkable. Just a sandstone blockade.

Jack reached out to steady himself on the wall to jump back down and suddenly he was falling through the wall!

I heard him hit the ground with a whomp!

His legs stuck out of solid rock.

"Whoa!" That was Jack's voice coming from within the rock. His legs shifted and Jack came scrambling back out of the wall. "You gotta see this!"

He leaped to his feet and the next thing I know, he plunges through the rock face. A second later, his hand reaches out of the wall and grabs me, pulling me through with him!

Chapter 3

The Discovery

W E STOOD IN A chamber the size of my parent's walk-in closet. From this side, we could see through the entrance, but if we stepped back out, we couldn't see in. When Jack did that a couple times, I realized something and told him to shut off his flashlight. Snapping them both off, instead of being in darkness, the chamber walls glowed faintly.

Once the novelty faded from what must have been a holographic(!) wall, we examined the other peculiar feature of the cave, only we didn't know what it was.

A platform of some kind? Or maybe a control center? The thing was made of a bluish plastic or maybe ceramic. The base was about a foot high and round, with a column at one end and a railing that came two-thirds around at just above waist level. Except for the railing, it looked like a really big weight scale at the doctor's office, only instead of the slidey weight thing, it was a display panel of some sort straight out of Star Trek, and the platform was big enough for four people to comfortably stand on. Which Jack promptly did.

"Don't go up there, Jack! You don't know what it is!"

"It's cool!" He ran his hands over the railing. "It's like a treadmill from the future!"

Okay, other than that, it was round and didn't have a rotating belt on the platform that was a better description than mine.

I climbed up there with Jack and did my own examination. The railing was featureless and warm to the touch. A wide display face topped the column. Faint lights played under whatever it was made of.

Jack started poking at the lights, and I grabbed his hands. I was ready to wet my pants and Jack was clearly elated, a huge smile on his face and mischief in his eyes.

In his excitement, he punched me in the arm and said, "To the moon, Alice!"

Something shimmered around us, and the platform rocketed through the cave with us in tow! Rock blurred as we flew past and we both screamed as we jetted out of the bigger cave entrance, rising faster and faster in the air!

TO THE MOON, ALICE!

I almost threw up as Kentucky fell below us and then it was the continent and then both North and South America and then it got dark all of a sudden and that was the Earth below us and it was shrinking and we kept screaming! I pinwheeled and started to fall backward, Jack reaching out to stop me from falling off the platform, but I bounced off something I couldn't see and was flung back onto my feet!

Jack started yelling again, pointing and oh my Lord, that was the moon and it was growing and the Earth was small behind us and the Moon was filling our vision, but then the platform spun around and we were looking into space!

We landed in a gray cloud of dust which seemed to linger in the air and Jack was jumping up and down, "We're on the Moon! We're on the Moon!"

And that's when I passed out.

Jack was shaking me and when my eyes fluttered open, he asked a very good question. "Why aren't we dead, Hud?"

I got to my feet, feeling shaky. Reaching out, my fingers came in contact with something that wasn't there. A force field? Beyond it laid the moonscape, a vast gray desert punctuated with craters.

I pinched myself, and nothing happened. So I pinched Jack hard, and he slugged my shoulder.

"What'd you do that for?" he said.

I shrugged. "I thought I must be dreaming, but pinching myself didn't do anything, so I thought maybe you were dreaming."

"Oh. Sorry for punching you."

"S'okay." I looked around. "Is that the moon rover?" I said, pointing. Off in the distance, through the gray silt that was still drifting back down from our landing, was a lump with tires. My glasses messed up my far vision, but I thought all those lumps were garbage left over from the Apollo missions that took place before we were born.

"I wonder if it still works?" Jack said.

"This can't be happening, Jack."

"I think it already did, Hud."

Just to make myself crazy, I took stock of all the things that should have killed us. "How long did that take, d'you think?"

"Five minutes, maybe?"

"So, first we should have been turned into paste from the acceleration, then burned up from friction, next suffocated from lack of oxygen, then exploded from being in space, frozen from being in space... anything I'm missing?"

"I think our eyes should be burned out by the sun with no atmosphere to filter it. Didn't the astronauts have gold visors or something?" See, Jack is a lot smarter than he looks; I hadn't thought of that.

"This thing is a spaceship," I said, patting the railings.

"Weird looking spaceship."

"Jack, what do we do now?"

He pondered that a moment and then smiled brightly. "Let's explore!"

I reached out and knocked on the nothing that surrounds us. Jack frowned and pushed on it.

"Jack, you get that there's no air out there, right?"

"I want to go out there!" he shouted.

The spaceship-thing vibrated slightly, and a panel opened on the face of the control panel where no panel had been before. A tray slid out with two bands on it, each about an inch wide and made of what looked like rubber and glass, but I suspected wasn't either.

"What are we supposed to do with those?" Jack said.

Before I could answer, a hologram projected from a jewel-like thing in the center of the tray. A hand appeared, plucking a holographic version of the band and slipping it on a skinny wrist.

My blood ran cold.

Not because of the holography; we'd both seen that a hundred times on TV and in movies. But because the hand wasn't a hand at all. At least not a human hand. It was longer, with an extra knuckle on each of the three fingers and a thumb on either side of them. No pinky, you understand, a thumb instead. And the hand, blue because the holographic beam was blue, slid the band onto its wrist with no help from another hand. The knuckles writhed like jointed snakes, moving the band into place.

Up to this point, we'd had no time to guess at where the platform came from. Now, unless the government had a weird sense of humor, it was clear aliens had made it.

What if they came back and found it missing?

"Alice, who made you?" Jack said.

"Alice?"

"She responded to, 'to the moon, Alice,' so that's her name."

"Her?"

"All ships are girls; didn't you know that?"

When we turned back to the hologram, it had changed. The hand had become the entire alien. There was no scale to tell if it was tall, but it looked tall because it was long and skinny. It had two arms, each with two elbows ending in that weird hand. It could probably scratch its first pair of knees without bending over. The head was longer than ours, but the features were similar, though the nose was so flat it almost spread across the whole face. Its clothes looked like a cross between biker shorts and a wrestling singlet.

I felt like I needed to sit down, but there was nowhere to sit.

"Where is he, Alice?" Apparently, Jack assumed all astronauts were men.

The hologram alien broke into a jillion pieces and blew away on an unseen wind.

"He's dead?" Jack asked.

Back to the hand with fingers curled and both thumbs up over the back of the hand. My thumb would have to be broken to go up like that.

"Does that mean Yes?" I asked.

Again, the double-thumbs up.

"How do you say No, Alice?" I said.

Two thumbs down in another position my thumb would never go.

"Can you speak, Alice?" Jack asked. He kept coming up with good questions.

Double-thumbs down. That struck me as odd.

"Why not?" I said.

The hologram showed Alice, then zoomed to the base. Suddenly, a bullet came into view and pierced through Alice's force field (shown by ripples in the air) and then into the base. The hologram zoomed again, showing us the bullet's path inside Alice, impacting a bead and breaking it.

"You're broken?"

Double-thumbs up.

"Can we fix you?"

Double-thumbs down.

"How did the bullet get through your force field?"

The hologram displayed the bullet, and equations scrolled down while models of atoms appeared.

Jack put it together. "Whatever it was made of could get through?"

Double-thumbs up.

"Who shot at you?" I asked.

The hologram morphed into something I hadn't expected. I'd been thinking a policeman or a soldier, but Alice was showing an Indian on horseback... sorry, a Native American on horseback... with an old-fashioned rifle in his hands.

"Huh?" Jack said.

"Was this, like, 200 years ago?"

Double-thumbs down.

"100 years ago?" I said.

One thumb up, one thumb down.

"Okay, around 100 years ago," I said.

Double-thumbs up.

"You've been alone a long time," Jack said.

The double-thumbs up remained.

"I'm sorry," Jack said. I guess he understood about loneliness.

The hologram showed the hand slipping on the bands again.

Jack looked at me, and I shrugged. We put on the wristbands.

They shrank to tightly wrap around our wrists, and then we both flinched at a stabbing pain.

"Hey!" Jack said, looking to punch something.

The pain went away and lights suddenly played behind the control panel.

"It won't come off!" Jack said, pulling at it.

The now-empty tray tilted up like a hand and shoved Jack off the platform! The force field had fallen and Jack was out there with no air!

"Cool!" he said.

"You can breathe?"

"Yeah! Come on out!" Jack was throwing moon dirt up... and up... it stretched high into the sky and seemed to only consider coming back down. It was cool! I was about to jump down when an important thought crossed my mind.

"Alice, are you going to stay here until we get back?"

Double-thumbs up.

"And you'll take us home when we ask?"

Still double-thumbs up.

"Thanks!" I said and jumped off the platform and immediately became disoriented! I'd expected to drop next to Jack, but instead, I was going up! Wait, now I was drifting down well beyond Jack!

Duh! Gravity is different here!

I touched down and bounced a little, rising back up and down again before settling in the gray lunar dust, which puffed up in greeting. I felt really weird. Light and strong at the same time.

"Careful, Jack! We have to move differently here!" Hey, wait a minute. "Jack, can you hear me?"

He bounced next to me. "Yeah."

"I'm pretty sure you can't hear when there's no air."

Jack raised his bracelet and shook it at me. "Communicator and force field generator in one!"

"And temperature control and air-maker. All that in this little thing?"

"The pinch must have been Alice figuring out what we needed."

Glancing over to Alice, a blue double-thumbs up appeared.

TO THE MOON, ALICE!

"How cool is this? Race you to the rover!" Jack yelled and turned to run, but found himself turning full circle instead.

"I told you, you have to move differently here. You weigh about twenty pounds and every movement is more powerful."

"Yes, teacher," Jack said, rolling his eyes. Turning more carefully, he smirked at me and took off. Or meant to. Instead, he was tumbling through the no-air, then rolling in the dust.

I experimented and after a few faulty, bouncy steps, I could make decent time, covering a couple of yards with each step. I made it to the rover upright. Jack tumbled next to me a few moments later.

The lunar rover our astronauts had left behind was bigger than it looked on TV. We didn't have the big, puffy spacesuits, so the proportions were off for us. Everything looked big partially because the horizon was so much closer and smaller than we were used to. The rover was little more than a couple of seats attached to a bare frame with huge tires, batteries, bins and a big satellite dish on the front, but compared to my scale model back home and to us, it was humongous.

"Think it still works?" Jack said.

It was covered in fine, gray silt that twinkled in the sun, though not as much as I'd have thought, considering it had been up here for a couple of decades.

"There might be some juice left in the batteries," I said.

"I wanna drive," Jack said. Fine with me. He was less likely to roll us over in a crater.

We settled into the seats. The controls were oversized to make it easy to operate with thick gloves, so they were huge in our hands.

"How do you start it?" Jack said.

We looked over the controls. "No key," I said.

"No switch, either. Maybe it's back here!" Jack said, turning around in his seat to look at the controls behind the seat. In doing so, he pressed the plate-sized pedals, and we lurched forward, plowing through the lunar dust.

"It must always be on!" I yelled, which wasn't necessary since no wind rushed by and the motor was silent. Jack fumbled back into his seat and grasped the T-shaped steering control between us.

The front left fender was gone, so dust and small rocks sifted down after being kicked up by the wheels. I looked over at Jack and saw him covered in dust, but none touched him. Our force fields were invisible, but clearly outlined by the moon "snowfall."

TO THE MOON, ALICE!

He eased up on the accelerator, and we bumped to a stop. It took several minutes for the dust to settle back to the moon and we watched it all trickle off our force fields.

Jack was smiling widely, and his eyes were brighter than the sun. I'm pretty sure mine were too.

"Hang on!" Jack yelled. He floored it and the buggy shot forward. Okay, "shot" might be an exaggeration since top speed was no faster than a running kid on Earth, but it seemed faster as we chewed up ground. The satellite dish waved in the breeze...

Wait, there was no breeze on the moon... I looked closer and saw a red light blinking on an old-fashioned camera housing. Oh, no! I scrambled forward and overshot. Backing up more carefully, I yanked the cable with all my strength and it popped out of the camera's housing. The red light winked off.

"What was that all about?" Jack asked.

"I think we just sent a TV signal to NASA."

"Whoops!" Jack said. "Hang on!"

I spun around and saw what Jack was heading for and yelled, "aaaahhhh" as we climbed up a small slope and over the edge... and kept climbing.

The buggy seemed to slowly realize that it couldn't fly and tipped over, giving us a view that the down slope was a lot steeper than expected! We bailed out as the rover heeled over, back over front.

Falling in slow motion takes a lot of the terror out of it. Jack somersaulted and simply crashed, absorbing the force with his shoulder. I flipped over and landed flat on my back.

It didn't hurt.

I took stock, and everything seemed to be okay.

Looking up, I saw that Jack had discovered the joy of gymnastics on the moon. His first hand-spring took him twenty feet and his landing and bounce threw him ten feet in the "air."

I wondered if you could jump off the moon, but dismissed that as silly and tried a standing back flip. Three revolutions later, I hit the ground on my back and bounced up, taking a while to find my feet.

"Hey, Hud, come over here," Jack said. That'll take some getting used to. Jack sounded like he was right beside me when he was actually standing on a big rock.

I skipped over to him and realized the rock was actually the casing of a collection bin. That wasn't what had awed Jack, however. Following his pointed finger, something monstrous and shiny hulked on the lunar flat.

"Is it alien, y'think?" Jack said.

I weighed my answer. Everything up here was alien in that humans were alien to the moon, but that wasn't what he was asking. It was like a gold tower far in the distance. "I don't know, Jack."

"Let's go find out!" and he was off at a bouncing, skipping run. I followed more cautiously. If it was alien-alien and not just human-alien, then they might still be there, and if they were there and no one on Earth knew it, then they were hiding on the moon and might do anything to keep their secret. On the other hand, if they were here secretly, having a big, shiny tower wasn't the best idea with the telescopes we had on Earth and in orbit.

I was concentrating on my moon-walking, so I was surprised when I heard Jack say, "Bummer." He was already at the tower and with him standing next to it, I realized it wasn't a tower. It wasn't that much taller than Jack, and it certainly wasn't as far away as it had looked. The screwy horizons had tricked our perceptions.

"It's one of ours," Jack lamented.

I'd forgotten that the astronaut's lunar lander was left behind with only the escape module taking off. What was left was a tripod scaffolding that was wrapped in gold foil with "U.S.A." in black written on the foil.

Jack tapped the gold foil, and it vibrated over the frame. "What's this?"

"Just what it looks like. Gold."

"Seriously? The real thing?"

"Yup."

Jack's eyes narrowed. "How do you know?"

"I went through a moon phase, remember? Models, dioramas, reports..."

"Geek stuff."

"Yeah, geek stuff."

"So it's valuable."

"Gold normally is."

"There's a lot here. We take this home and we're rich!"

"Not as much as it looks. It's really thin."

"Makes it easy to crunch into a ball. Let's take it!"

It's not like anyone would miss it. There had to be several Earth-pounds of it. That was a lot of money. Wait. "What if it's radioactive?" I said.

"Why would it be?"

"You know, it's in unprotected space. There's radioactivity out here, I think."

"Why aren't we radioactive, then? We'd get sick, wouldn't we?"

"The wristbands, I guess."

"We gonna tell anybody about this, Hud?"

"I dunno. This is a pretty big deal. The government would want to take Alice apart to see how she works."

"That's not cool."

"Maybe we should head back and make sure we can get back home. We can figure it out there."

"Yeah, okay..." his voice trailed off as he looked over my shoulder. I turned to see and my breath whooshed out of me.

The Earth was rising over the horizon, and it was awesome!

It came up pretty fast, taking up a quarter of the horizon. At first, it looked like it was really close, but after a while, we could see the night-side of Earth as if space was slowly eating it. It appeared to shrink and the realization that our blue, white, green and brown planet had quite far away seized us.

"We should get home," I said, not taking my eyes off the Earth.

"We're not telling anyone about this," Jack said, equally entranced.

We finally tore our eyes away from that magnificent sight and realized how dumb we were. We'd taken our eyes off Alice and were completely lost. Direction had no meaning here. What was East or West on the moon? Every direction looked completely the same. Human garbage left over from missions and crashed probes from several countries cropped up here and there, but no Alice. I wasn't going to cry in front of Jack, but I was hungry and lost and I had to go to the bathroom.

Jack was in explorer mode, so he had the inscrutable expression that would suffer no tears. Just as my lower lip started to tremble, Jack snapped his fingers.

"Maybe she comes when called," he said.

"Alice!" I bawled.

He glowered at me. Raising his wristband to his lips, he said, "Alice, could you come get us, please?"

I held my breath as we scanned the surrounding sky. Jack shot a finger out, pointing. Alice was cruising over the landscape, plumes of dust rising behind her.

We whooped and hollered as she arrowed toward us. All the jumping—that took us yards in the air—was a mistake.

"I gotta pee," I said.

"Go ahead, Hud. Write your name on the moon," Jack said.

"In a force field?"

"Well, that would be nasty."

"I really gotta go!"

"You're gonna have to hold it, partner."

Alice settled in the dust beside us. I was clenching my jaw in concentration.

"All aboard!" shouted Jack. He hopped up. I gently climbed on.

TO THE MOON, ALICE!

"Take us home, Alice!"

Alice shot into the air, easily escaping the Moon's pull. Sudden vertigo almost made me unclench, but I managed to hold it, barely.

We sailed through space with Earth growing rapidly before us. I imagined the Space Shuttle on re-entry, appearing on fire, and hoped Alice would slow down enough to prevent us from cooking, but she didn't. The Earth was giant now, consuming space in front of us. I felt us pierce atmosphere as the air within our force field thickened ever-so slightly. No flames marked our passage despite our speed.

As the ground rushed toward us, I gripped the railing hard, then Alice flipped over as she settled into the woods and slid back into her cave and behind her hologram wall.

The second we touched down, I sprinted off and through the cave in tight steps.

"Try to make it out of the cave!" called Jack.

Yeah, good luck with that.

Five minutes and much relief later, I rejoined Jack in Alice's hideout. Jack was examining Alice.

"Find anything?" I asked.

Jack pointed at her base. "There's the bullet hole."

"Alice, did that break anything else?"

A hologram jewel rose to the surface of her control panel and projected a double-thumbs down.

"Are there a lot of things that can get through your force field?"

Double-thumbs down again.

"Hud, what were bullets made of back then?"

"Um, lead, I guess?"

"Was it lead, Alice?"

Double-thumbs down.

"Steel?"

Double-thumbs down.

"Hud, what else were bullets made of?"

"Iron, Alice?"

Double-thumbs down.

"Ooo! I know! Silver bullets!"

"No one used silver bullets, Jack."

"Vampire hunters did."

"No such thing as vampires, Jack."

"This morning you wouldn't say double jointed, two-thumbed aliens existed."

"Point taken."

"Besides, the Lone Ranger used silver bullets."

"Alice, was it silver?"

Double-thumbs up.

"Seriously? Silver bullets?"

"You were shot by Tonto?" asked Jack.

The holo-hand turned over, palm up, with both thumbs crossed.

"What's that mean?" Jack asked.

"I don't know," I said.

Double-thumbs up.

"Huh! Thumbs crossed means I don't know."

The cave had gotten darker, which meant the sun was going down.

"We have to get home, Jack."

"Yeah. We'll be back tomorrow, Alice."

"I got church in the morning."

"So, come out and join me when you're done."

"Huh-uh, no way. We come out together or not at all."

"What for?"

"Because!"

"Okay, okay."

"Let's go."

"Sure, in a minute."

"Now, Jack."

"Fine!"

He followed me out of her holo hideout and turned back. "Thanks, Alice. Sorry you've been alone so long and that you were hurt."

He looked at me, prompting.

"Uh, thanks, Alice," I said.

With a longing look, Jack said, "We'll be back, promise."

A double-thumbs up responded.

Tramping through the woods as the afternoon darkened, what we had just done seemed like a dream.

"We were on the moon," Jack whispered.

"Yeah," I agreed.

"How far do you think she can go?"

"I don't know. Pretty far, I guess, if she brought that alien here."

"Where do you think he's from?"

"Far away, I'd guess. No life in our solar system other than Earth."

"You sure?"

"Yeah. Well, no, but where else? I'd think we'd know if Mars or Venus had life and the others are made of gas, so that's a no-go."

"Don't those have moons?"

"I'd still think we'd detect, like, radio waves or something."

"Why do you suppose nobody came to get Alice?"

"Maybe they still will."

"Huh, hadn't thought of that."

We walked on in silence for a while.

"We need rules," Jack said.

I was thinking the same things. "Okay, no trips alone."

"And no one else! This is our secret."

"Yeah, I'm good with that."

"Maybe we should move her. You know, closer to us. This is a long walk."

"My house, maybe?" I said.

"No way. Your dad can sniff tech. He's a bigger geek than you are!"

"Yeah, good point.

Jack smacked my shoulder. "Oh, duh! We don't have to go to her, she can come to us!" He held up his wristband. I looked at mine. We'd forgotten to take them off.

"Maybe we should take these back," I said.

Jack lifted the band to his lips. "Hey, Alice, can we keep the wristbands?"

A jewel the size of a wart raised on Jack's wristband and a tiny holographic double-thumbs up appeared.

How cool was that?

Jack stayed for dinner, as he always did on Saturday nights. Saturdays were not good evenings at the Taylor home. The only reason Jack's dad made it home Saturday nights was if he didn't have enough money to stay out and pass out, which put him in a brutal mood. Best for Jack to remain with us as late as possible. He was welcome to spend the night, of course, but that would mean joining us at church Sunday morning, which Jack was dead-set against. He'd rather sneak in late and take his chances with his dad. I didn't think that was fair. Our church was actually a lot of fun.

We got back later than we should have, but fortunately, Mom was making pepperoni spaghetti, which only got better the longer you cooked it. Flour dusted the kitchen and Mom's hair. That meant the noodles were homemade, cooked fast, and tasted terrific.

At school, our Home Ec teacher floated around the appliances and made cooking look simple and fun. Mom wasn't like that. The story goes that she had never cooked anything before marrying Dad, and not much thereafter until I came along. Then, Dad liked to say, everything changed. Mom believed that a mother should cook. "Not a wife, mind you," Dad would say, "so be grateful!"

Mom tackled cooking like she did everything else; full force and with full mastery. I wasn't even old enough to eat proper food when she started that kick, so Dad put on a lot of weight. As good as she was, though, she never enjoyed it. No floating amongst the appliance, rather divide and conquer. "She's the same way with computer code, son," Dad would say. "She saves all her warmth and joy for relationships." I didn't really know what that meant, but Dad said it a lot. I think it means she really likes people, unlike most computer nerds. She's just good at everything and computering paid the best, I guess.

Mom had a shelf of cookbooks. She never made anything without a recipe and never varied from it. Dad had his favorite books, Joy of Cooking, to which Mom says, "It's no such thing!" and anything by Betty Crocker. Jack and I love the Italian cookbooks and that was what was on the counter.

"You're late!" Dad said, looking up from the newspaper. "I've been salivating for an hour."

"Sorry, Dad." My own mouth was awash with hunger as the Italian aroma sank into every pore.

"Nothing for it. Go wash up."

"Where's Ela?" Jack asked. He had a soft spot for her.

Dad's eyes widened as he realized it was his job to watch her and he had no idea where she was.

"Over here, Jack, in the laundry basket," Mom said, wiping flour from her forehead but only adding more.

"I knew that," Dad said.

"Uh-huh," Mom said.

Ela had a thing for fresh laundry. Whenever she fussed in Mom's arms, she'd plop the baby into the laundry basket and Ela would calm right down. Mom did a lot of laundry.

Jack beelined for the baby.

"Wash!" Mom said.

He veered off to the laundry room deep sink, and I joined him, washing to the elbows because Mom would check.

Freshly scrubbed, Jack gently scooped Ela out of the basket. She burped at him and he laughed. It was a side of him I only saw with my sister, and as mushy as it was, I liked it.

After inspection, Ela was squeezed into her car carrier (something else she really liked) and lashed to a chair.

Perfect spaghetti filled our plates garnished by fresh-baked bread. Jack always had the look of Christmas when Mom served him, no matter what it was. It was all I could do to wait for grace before digging in.

We all held hands, and Dad must have been hungry because his prayer was short.

There was no talking, just the clinking of forks on plates and groans of pleasure for several bites before Mom put a happy stop to it. "You're welcome, already!" and we all laughed.

"What were you guys up to all day?" Dad asked.

"Went to the moon, Mr. Cook!" Jack said.

I laser-eyed him, but he only smiled.

"No wonder you're so late; that's quite a trip," Dad said.

"Should have brought back some cheese," Mom said.

We looked at her blankly.

TO THE MOON, ALICE!

"You know, the moon's made of cheese," Mom said, a little crossly. For a people-person, her jokes never worked.

"The astronauts must have ate it all, Mrs. Cook," Jack said.

Dad and I laughed. Mom pursed her lips. "Eaten, dear."

"Yours was funny, too, Janet," Dad said.

"Eat your spaghetti."

"Yes, dear," Dad said. "Think you'll go back tomorrow?"

"I was thinking Mars, Mr. Cook, or maybe Venus."

"Oh, no, Jack, Venus is for ladies."

"Mars it is, then!"

"Why is Venus for ladies, Dad?"

"Oh, you know. Mars is for men because it's red and angry looking, while Venus is clouded in mystery, just like a woman. It's also stormy and dangerous. Mars is your better bet."

"Is that how you see me, Daniel? Stormy and dangerous?" Mom growled.

With her face smudged with flour and eyes practically glowing, she did look stormy. We all did our best not to laugh, but our mouths trembled with the effort. She simmered.

"This is the best spaghetti ever, Mrs. Cook," Jack managed.

"Nice try, Jack, but you're all in the doghouse."

"Pluto!" we chorused, and even Mom laughed.

Despite all the talk of moons and planets, kids and adults really did seem like they lived on different worlds in different orbits. Mom and Dad had talked about homeschooling me but decided public school offered greater "rounding," whatever that meant. As a result, I had a whole life apart from them, just as they had their work lives apart from me. I think they are just as clueless about my school life as I am about their work. They wanted me to study art and English and their own beloved science, but I'm sure they'd be horrified by what school is really like. I know they went, themselves, but that was a long time ago.

Here we were, having two completely different conversations; Dad thinking we're imagining things and us completely serious. It shouldn't surprise me, though. A lot of our conversations go like this.

Like the discussion we had about drugs last week when Dad wanted to know how aware I was of things like that. Sure, I'm aware. Kids sold or shared all sorts of drugs. Every kid knew who they could go to and who to stay away from. This one kid in my homeroom is considered ADHD, so his parents have him taking all sorts of prescriptions. But he doesn't take them, he sells them to the brainy kids who want to be brainier. There's even a kid from church who dips into his parent's prescription drugs. All I told my dad was, "Yeah, I know." And he asks if I'm smart enough to stay away from them, which I am and I say so, but I also know the kids who do use them say the same thing.

These kinds of things bother me. I'd talk to Jack about it, but that wouldn't be fair. He doesn't have any kind of conversation with his dad. Still, Jack's like me. He doesn't do the dumb stuff. Maybe he would someday, his dad being an alcoholic and all, but right now he didn't.

So, Mom and Dad talk about drugs and bullying and the other things too dangerous to be involved in, and I reassure them I'm okay, and I am, but I also don't tell them about what goes on at school, things that would make them worry.

I don't know who I'm protecting, me or them.

Instead, we're talking about planets as if it's fun and games, but now, all of a sudden, we really can go to those places and this isn't a conversation of fun but a fact-finding mission so we can do things they'd never let us do if they knew.

I wonder if that's going to bother me?

"Could there be life on Venus, Mr. Cook?"

"Why don't you ask Mrs. Cook, Jack? I'll help you with Mars."

"Well, Mom?" I said.

She twirled spaghetti on her fork and considered. "Depends on what you mean by life."

"It's not a trick question, Mom."

"But it is. Are you talking about people or intelligent life? Or animals, which are complex but not intelligent? No, there almost certainly isn't on Venus. But simple or microscopic life, like mold, bacteria or such things? It could be."

"Do you think there's people like us on different planets?" We knew the answer better than they did, but I wanted to know what they thought.

Dad sighed and smiled at Mom. That was his way of saying he and Mom have talked about that a lot and that they disagreed.

"I love the idea of extraterrestrial life, and there is such life, I believe, in that God, angels and demons are extraterrestrial, but people like us out there? Would God make other people? I don't know. The Bible doesn't say so, except for extreme interpretations," he said.

"But it doesn't rule it out, either," Mom pointed out. "I sit under the stars and I'm filled with wonder. Mostly because God made all that, but also because of how wonderful it would be to meet people who lived around those stars."

TO THE MOON, ALICE!

"When I look at the stars, it makes me think about zit cream," Dad said.

Mom rolled her eyes and loudly crunched a piece of bread in protest.

"Maybe they're bad guys," Jack said.

"Mmmmm," Dad said. "The age-old question: would aliens able to make it all the way here be enlightened or conquerors?"

"What are we, Mr. Cook?"

"A bit of both, Jack. So, I suppose they could be, too. Only one way to find out, though. They'd have to come here and I don't see that happening."

"Or we could go there, Mr. Cook."

"You got a spaceship in your pocket, Jack?"

"How cool would that be?" Jack answered without answering.

Dad squinted his eyes at my wrist. "What's with the wristbands?"

Before I could come up with a convincing lie, or even decide if I wanted to lie, Jack offered the most disconcerting lie of all: the truth.

"That's how we stay in touch with our spaceship, Mr. Cook."

Dad had accepted that explanation with a concession to imagination and left it alone. Hours later we bid Jack, who as usual turned down a ride home, a good night.

Still later, I found myself unable to sleep. The craziness of being on the moon raced through my brain, but so did something else. Somehow, using the truth as a lie was bothering me.

My parents weren't like Jack's dad. They were fun, a little nerdy and included me in all their conversations if I was around. Unlike a lot of parents, they never talked down to me. I never believed in Santa Claus or the Easter Bunny, Mom and Dad had explained them as happy fictions from the beginning. "We'll never hold back the truth," they'd say, "so when we tell you about God, you'll have no reason to doubt us."

They were honest with me, and up until Middle School, I'd always been honest with them. Oh, sure, little lies before that, really transparent lies… "Did you break the lamp?" "Who, me?" But the real stuff, the things-parents-should-know stuff, I'd always been up front about. Dad could get angry and shout sometimes, but it wasn't like I didn't have it coming.

Then Middle School, and things got weird. I didn't talk about the changes going on with me unless prompted and then only enough to keep them happy. No way

I'd talk about the thoughts girls brought about. And then there was stuff that went on at school. I think there's an unspoken understanding among kids that if our parents—the ones who cared, anyway—had any clue about what really went on at school, would feel terribly guilty.

I remember in sixth grade, a couple weeks in, our youth pastor was preaching about Daniel and the lion's den and spent a long time trying to relate how Daniel felt. He could have saved his breath; as a new middle-schooler, I knew exactly how he felt, except God delivered Daniel and I had to go back to the lions every day.

The guy who said, "sticks and stones will break my bones but words will never hurt me" must have been homeschooled. The first week of sixth grade, my vocabulary skyrocketed with words my parents would never let me say. I was called horrible names and my mother was called horrible names! One of our first units in Social Studies was on the importance of maintaining high self-esteem. Jack and I had a good laugh after that class.

Every day when I get home from school, Mom asks how did it go? I always say, "Fine," which, if taken on balance, is true. Some of school can be fun when it isn't terrifying or boring. That first time, I remember making a conscious decision to not tell Mom anything that would bother her that she couldn't fix. It's called a lie of omission. I tell—or don't tell—a lot of those. Like the first time I was kidney-punched by Pruit, or the Atomic Wedgies the big kids take pride in giving to the little kids. Or when Mary Schmidt gave me a note that made me blush for weeks. Once, our Social Studies teacher had an emotional breakdown the day after President Obama was elected. She cried and blubbered, and none of us knew if she was happy or sad about it. No one told their parents or any other teachers, which is funny. There's a severity scale in every kid's mind. If Mr. Tompkins slams his finger in a drawer and swears his head off, everyone will know about it within a single period and all parents would be informed instantly when kids got home. But if Mr. Tompkins were to break into tears all period for no apparent reason, all the kids would know but no adults would.

The result is, I'm one person at school and another at home and church. The gap between those two persons is filled with lies, and the more lies told, the bigger the gap.

Maybe other kids don't see it, but I do, and it bothers me. As a little kid, I didn't weigh what I would or wouldn't tell Mom and Dad. Now I do. What if I weigh wrong?

Chapter 4

Touring the Solar System

I LIKE CHURCH.

We're small as churches go. Up until last year, we met in a former grocery store partitioned off into classrooms under the Produce and Bakery signs, offices in the former Frozen Foods area, and the sanctuary taking up what had been all the middle aisles.

Now we meet in our new church building, which is a small but proper church that smelled like new carpet.

I'd dreamed about meeting a mummified alien last night and welcomed worship to chase away the cobwebs of that dream.

Our band was loud and worship could get energetic with arms raised and people swaying. Mom sang well, Dad didn't, but didn't care, and I could do okay, I think.

Today I sang along but found my mind wandering to the afternoon's adventure. Where would we go? The songs were all familiar, so I could sing without thinking about it. Then I wondered how many other people were doing that? Were the words as important as feeling the worship? Did aliens sing? Did they believe in God? Should I ask if I see one? What will I do if I see one?

Sunday School was even harder. The little kids met in classes on the first floor, but the big kids were upstairs in a smaller, more fun sanctuary. Instead of plastic seats, we had cast-off furniture. Deep couches reserved for kids who wouldn't fall asleep, arm chairs of cloth, leather, and vinyl for the rest of us. It was awesome, so much better than the produce section.

Our youth pastor was a good guy, "just call me Kevin." Kevin kind of acted like one of us, but his music references were old and his hairline was crawling to the back of his head. He also had a paunch, which he didn't have when he started out. It came from his fabled Malt Talks (a "malt" is a milkshake, we found out). He'd use the ice cream to bribe us into meeting him one-on-one at a local restaurant where we'd talk about Jesus and stuff while sucking down milkshakes.

Sundays, though, he preached, but not like Pastor Matthews did downstairs. He asked a lot of questions and wanted real answers, so the kids talked as much as he did. Often, that would have great results and sometimes it would just fall into weirdness. Like today.

"Who here believes in people from outer space?" he said, snapping me out of my thoughts.

"Y'mean aliens?" asked a kid.

"Yep."

A few hands went up. I tentatively raised mine.

"I bring it up because something happened on the moon yesterday."

I felt my eyes go wide.

"Our moon?" the same kid asked.

"Yes, Mort, our moon," Kevin said.

"Because technically, our moon isn't in outer space," Mort said.

"Give me some leeway here, Mort. Yesterday, much to NASA's surprise, they received images from the moon. Seems the Lunar Buggy lit up and drove itself somehow and its camera caught the action and beamed it to Houston."

"Awesome!" Mort said.

"What did they see?" I asked, trying to keep the tremors out of my voice.

"Did they see aliens?" another kid said.

71

"Not specifically, but there were some interesting shadows. Let me show you." Kevin thumbed on the big, flat-screen TV that was already hooked up to his laptop.

A black-and-white grainy picture of the moon with what I knew was a strut on the buggy flashed on-screen. The sun cast a long shadow of the buggy onto the ground in front of it. In the shadow were two stretched people-looking shadows. Me and Jack.

"Kewl!" shouted a kid.

"Photoshop," smirked Mort.

"Pattern recognition," said Kevin.

"Huh?"

"Humans are pattern recognition machines. Show us a blob on toast and we see the Madonna, or here, we see shadows of seats and see people. Some people think we see things that aren't there because of pattern recognition. I believe we often see things that are there due to pattern recognition. That is, we have pattern recognition because we're expected, by God, to see patterns."

"How did the Lunar Rover–not 'buggy,' Kevin—get lit up?" Mort asked.

"Who knows? A radiation spike? Corrosion closed the solenoid? A dozen plausible explanations, really, but the one that intrigues all of us, did aliens do it?"

"Did they?" asked a girl from the couch.

"No, Beth, aliens didn't do it. But maybe angels did!"

A lot of the kids scoffed at that.

"Thank you. That's the reaction I was expecting. No, angels didn't take the Lunar Rover for a ride, but many of you were open to the idea of aliens, but not of angels. I'd like to examine that," Kevin said.

And that's what we did for the next hour, discussing Heaven, eternity, and outer space and dimensions. Normally, I'd eat this stuff up, but I fell into exactly what Kevin warned us against early in the sermon: "Don't get caught up in the example and miss the application." I was definitely stuck on the example, and it made getting back to Alice more exciting.

Finally, church was over and I goaded my parents to leave quickly instead of hanging out. Lunch was McDonald's, and I ate quickly. Unfortunately, no one else did.

"What is your hurry, Hudson?" Mom asked.

"Jack's waiting for me, Mom!"

"Jack has always waited before, son," Dad said.

"Yes, sir...," I growled.

Finally, I was at Jack's house. I'd debated taking my bike, but no telling what mood Jack's dad was in so I didn't risk having it sold while we were orbiting Mars or something.

Now that I was here, I was presented with the same old problem. How to let Jack know? I'd made the mistake of knocking on the door once. Mr. Taylor had scared me so badly I didn't come back for a month. Other times I rapped on Jack's bedroom window, but his dad didn't always pass out on his own bed Saturday nights. Jack would come home to find nowhere to sleep.

Typically, I paced outside his room, and Jack would eventually notice. I didn't want to lose any time today, though, so I debated.

Suddenly, my wrist vibrated. Jack's voice came out of my sleeve. "Out back, dufus."

The wristband was a cell phone!

I sprinted around the house and waded through the high grass to the crumbling barn. Or maybe it was a stable. Size-wise, it was in-between the two, like a midget barn or a stable with ambitions. It might have been painted once, but the boards were so old and weathered, the color was long gone.

I'm not a fan of spiders, so I ducked through the door, dangling from a single hinge with reluctance.

Sunlight filtered through cracks in the ceiling and walls, but my eyes still had to adjust. When they did, Alice stood shining in the dust-filled air, her control stalk toward me.

"Jack, you were supposed to wait for me!" I looked around. "Jack?"

"Up here!"

TO THE MOON, ALICE!

The beam Jack stood on looked rotting and dangerous, maybe 16 feet off the floor. "What are you doing? Get down here!"

Jack grinned and bent at the knees. "No!" I yelled as he launched into space. Jack plummeted like a rock, but before he struck the ground, his force field flared, cushioning his body as it hit the ground. Jack sprang up like a jack-in-the-box, that grin never fading as my heart tried to slow from its rapid beating. I slugged him and the field glowed in the dim light.

"It's cool, Hud. No pain!"

"No gain," I finished. "You were supposed to wait for me!" The field flared again as I slugged his other arm.

"No promises were broken, Hud. I got to thinking how long it would take to hike to her, so this morning when it was still dark, I called her to me! And she came! We've been talking while we waited for you."

"Talking?"

"You know, me talking, her thumbing and holoing."

"Holoing?"

"Yeah! Check this out. Alice, where are you from?"

The barn lit up with a cool blue light as a holo-display of the galaxy filled the space between us. The familiar spiral-arms of the Milky Way tilted from floor to ceiling.

"Mark Earth, please, Alice," Jack said.

Midway out on a tentacle of stars, a light pulsed. Earth.

"Now show us your planet," Jack said.

The room seemed to spin as the galaxy rotated. A light pulsed two spirals over from us, also midway up its length.

"I think that's a really long way," I said.

"Yeah. Want to see something really amazing? Alice, can you show us our solar system?"

I almost fell over from vertigo as the galaxy spun and enlarged!

The sun blazed in blue flames in the center of the barn. It was really bright and maybe two feet across. I put a hand up to block the light, but Alice dimmed it so we could see the planets and each of their moons orbiting it. Jupiter was the size of a softball, Saturn, and Neptune a bit smaller. Wait. I did a quick count.

"There are too many planets. This isn't our system."

"Alice, delete Mercury through Pluto."

"Pluto's not a planet."

"Shhh, watch," he said, pointing behind us.

A tiny orb the size of a pea pulsed into existence—Pluto—and winked out, taking the other eight planets with it. Two planets remained, one beyond Pluto, the other closer to the sun than Mercury.

"That doesn't make sense," I said.

"Sure it does. That one is so far out we can't see it from here, and this one..." he took a few steps to point at the one near the sun, "...will make sense in a second. Alice, bring back the other planets and include orbits."

Great rings circled the sun, passing through the planets, indicating their paths around the sun, including the far planet, though it was a lot farther out than Pluto was to the sun. I turned to the second one and its orbit was way different.

"Alice, shrink to include all orbits."

The sun dwindled to the size of a golf ball and the planets tightened ranks around it in sizes ranging from peas to b.b.'s. All but the weird planet's orbits were tight and circular, but the weird planet formed a giant oval that stretched way out to the walls of the barn.

"Show where they all are now."

Planets swirled from an orderly progression to places around the room. The rogue planet backed up over half way to the wall, far from the sun.

"Alice, animate to show the passage of time, one Earth year for every five seconds."

The planets launched from immobility to rapid movement. The rogue planet inched slowly toward the sun while the other planets spun around it quickly.

"It took me a long time to figure out the right year-per-second rate. I figure we'll be able to see that planet when we're old men."

"Can I do one?" I said.

"Sure."

"Alice, can you show where life appears in our solar system?"

The Earth lit up brightly and further out, two moons, one around Jupiter and the other around Saturn, throbbed weakly.

"Alice, can you widen out to show us life in the galaxy?"

I steeled myself as the image adjusted back to the galaxy view. Up and down each tentacle, light pulsed, brighter in some places, weaker in others.

Remembering our conversation from last night, I adjusted my command.

"Alice, show only intelligent life."

The extra light winked out. Our solar system, except for Earth, went dark while farther up the galactic arm, two places blinked. Four other arms, all mid-way up, also blinked in a few places. All in all, for something as big as the galaxy, less than a dozen lights blinked.

"Hey, wait, what did your mom say last night? What did she call non-intelligent life that wasn't like teeny stuff?"

"Y'mean animals? Um, complex life, I think."

TO THE MOON, ALICE!

"Alice!" Jack said, "Show us non-intelligent complex life in our solar system."

The solar system spun into view, but the pulsing light was only on Earth. So, the other stuff on the two gas-giant moons was bacteria or something. "Now in the galaxy, Alice," I said.

Another spin out to the galaxy level and light pulsed along every arm, nowhere near as much as micro-life, but a lot more than just intelligent life.

"Delete places with insects and spider-things only."

Over half the lights winked out.

Jack suddenly smiled. "Show only planets with dinosaur-like things!"

Lights rearranged so that six planets on three arms blinked.

"That's where I want to go!" Jack said.

"Wait, Jack, that's a long, long way away. We only have a few hours!"

"So, we skip school tomorrow."

"My parents would kinda notice, Jack."

"Mine wouldn't."

"We said we'd only go together."

Jack simmered for a moment, then brightened. "Alice, how long would it take to get to the closest dino-planet?"

Alice apparently didn't know about clocks or calendars. The galactic display winked out, and the Earth appeared as big as a basketball in front of us. Sections scrolled over the Earth, like wedges of an orange... or like the number positions on a clock. I counted 25 sections. "Each of those sections is just under an hour, I think."

One section divided into ten smaller sections, with four of them colored in. Maybe Alice understood clocks better than we did.

Jack and I looked at each other. I pointed at the non-colored sections. "Is that how long it would take?"

A line drew itself across the colored sections.

"It would take, what, twenty minutes? How is that possible? It took five minutes to go from here to the moon!" I said. "That planet is like a billion times farther than the moon!"

To answer, Alice displayed the moon in place around the Earth and we watched Alice with us aboard rise straight from Earth to the Moon.

Then she displayed the galaxy again, in 3-D, and dramatically flattened it like it was on a paper map.

Jack and I looked at each other again. Where was she going with this?

When we didn't say anything, she "snapped" the map, almost impatiently.

"Okay, okay, it's the galaxy, we get it."

Next, Alice changed the map from flat to a ruffled shape, the fabric of the galaxy folding back and forth on itself. Alice made an ant-sized holo-copy of herself coming off the sectioned Earth and traveled up and down across the folded map with the colored sections of the Earth spinning from colored to non-colored, simulating days and days of time. The holo-Alice reversed herself and came back to the spinning Earth and this time she passed through the ridges of the galactic map in a straight line, stopping on the dino-planet with an elapsed time of twenty minutes on the Earth segments.

"Are you saying space is folded?"

Two thumbs up.

Jack shouted, "Let's go!"

I had to agree.

I still screamed like a little girl when we shot through the atmosphere to space. Jack pretended not to notice, because that's the kind of friend he is.

We hovered over the Earth, watching half a dozen satellites whiz by underneath us. I wasn't sure if Alice was just giving us a moment to enjoy the best view of our lives or if it took some time to build to warp drive, or whatever it was. Watching Europe and part of Africa gave me sudden inspiration.

"Wait!" I cried.

"What?" asked Jack.

"The dino-planet is a must-see, Jack, but so is our solar system! Hey, Alice, could you take us on a tour of the solar system and back home in four hours?"

"I wanna see a T-Rex!"

"We will, Jack, honest! But haven't you ever wanted to see Jupiter or Saturn? Maybe we could check out the micro-life on those moons! Please, Jack?"

"We'd have to wait until next weekend to go anywhere else, Hud. Think about it, a real, live Jurassic Park!"

"Summer break is in a few weeks. We have months to go where we want!"

"Fine, fine, have it your way."

"You won't regret it, Jack."

Jack didn't, but I almost did.

Alice took off through space. She didn't use rockets or visible propulsion of any kind. We only knew we were moving because the Earth shrank drastically. Soon it was out of sight entirely and the sun was noticeably smaller. Then if felt as if we weren't moving at all. There was nothing to see except for the dwindling sun and sparkling stars, brighter than anything, but with far less warmth than the sun. I felt colder even though Alice kept the temperature constant and comfortable.

"Hey, what's that?" Jack said, pointing.

I looked but couldn't see anything. And then I could. Sort of. It looked like space was shimmering. We must have been going really fast because suddenly the shimmering wasn't shimmering, it was first gravel hanging in space and then boulders and all of a sudden, they were giant asteroids and we were diving right into them!

I hadn't realized Alice was luminous. Or maybe she had headlights... great cliffs of rock would light up as we almost skimmed them and then it spun away behind us, only to be replaced by a monster in front of us! Alice jinked and weaved until my stomach threatened to revolt.

Jack was whooping it up like he was having the time of his life while I was trying to figure out what would happen to vomit in a force field.

And then we were out of the asteroid field, leaving it far behind. My mouth went dry as I saw what was up ahead.

Glowing in the black ink of space was an amazing sight.

"That's Saturn," Jack said, noticing the pale rings.

It went from disk to awesome planet in seconds.

"That's not Saturn, Jack, it's Jupiter!"

"But the rings," he said.

"Jupiter has rings, you just can't see them from Earth."

"But they're huge!"

We'd come in above—or was that below?—the gas giant. Alice climbed up—or down—the face of Jupiter and the rings shifted from a beautiful pale band to giant boulders floating in space. It was awesome. Moons that looked like pebbles chased their shadows on the planet below like balloons on a slow breeze.

I'd seen pictures, of course. I knew the great red spot was a never-ending storm. I even knew Jupiter was a gas planet, but to actually see it! It was gigantic! Moons circled with their shadows dotting the gaseous surface. As vast as Jupiter was, black space was even more vast! Stuck on the face of our planet, I'd never known the emptiness and grandeur of space's nothingness. Jupiter gave off — reflected? — so much light that the stars were invisible. The isolation of the king-size planet tore at something I didn't know was inside me.

According to our astronomy unit, Jupiter was named after Jove, the Roman counterpart to Zeus, the king of the gods. Now I understood! I wanted to fall to my knees at the glory of this planet!

I must have because I had to look up at Jack when he said, "What?"

I felt so small! So overwhelmed by beauty! How could he not see it? For the first time in my life, I understood what it was to worship. Not Jove, not the planet, but the maker of the planet! Alice had taken station above the rings. Jupiter was so vast that beneath us the boulders were distinct, yet as they stretched ever further around the planet, they blurred into the illusion of a solid band again.

Jack had given up on me, placing elbows on Alice's encircling arms. He gaped while I melted.

I remember being fascinated by my fingerprints as a little boy, amazed by the detail in such a small area. This was the opposite of that feeling. Even with nothing to compare it to for scale, its enormity pressed in on me like the gravity Alice wasn't letting us feel.

"God made this!" I breathed.

"Huh? Yeah, okay, whatever," Jack said and turned back to the sight.

All my life, I've known Jack and in so many ways he was superior to me, but for the first time, I could comprehend the difference between us. As bad a Christian as I was, never taking the time to really read my Bible or pray, I knew who made all of this and so I could appreciate it for what it was. Jack saw a planet; I saw God's awesome glory!

Maybe that was the moment when things started to go badly for us. It wouldn't be obvious for a long time off, but looking back, I bet that's when it began.

There would be a day far in the future when I'd wished we'd never found Alice, but staring at Jupiter, finally coming into my faith, I thought Alice was the best gift I'd ever been given. How wrong I was.

"I take it back. THESE are RINGS!" Jack shouted.

We'd moved on from Jupiter and saw Neptune and Uranus next. We weren't sure which was which because neither planet was the same color as in our astronomy books. I'm not sure how to say this... they weren't as bright, but they were far richer colors and something you just couldn't see from Earth was how the surface of the gas giants swirled and their thin rings swam like fish around them. In books and even in the films we'd seen, these majestic planets just seemed to sit there in their gravity wells doing nothing. Not so. They were as active as flames in a campfire. Jack must have been thinking the same thing.

"You suppose if we dropped a match they'd light up?"

"Pretty sure we'd get in trouble for that."

And so we'd moved on to Saturn, which took a while. We realized Alice had taken us to the planets most in line with Earth from the sun; those "closest" to us. Saturn was now on the other side of the solar system. It must have taken Alice twenty minutes to get there. My mind boggled at the speed that must have taken, yet we felt nothing in the cocoon of her force field.

TO THE MOON, ALICE!

We'd thought Jupiter's rings had been amazing! Jack's outburst came when we were still way far out from the beautiful planet. Her rings throbbed with reflected light and as we grew closer, individual asteroid-sized rocks flashing like diamonds.

Saturn's rings stretched out wider and deeper than Jupiter's or Neptune's (I think it was Neptune!). The boulders that made up each ring were of different sizes, distances apart, and probably what they were made of. As a result, the swirling rings were a riot of colors and textures.

I'd fallen to my knees again. Even as I looked at this cosmic sight and felt dwarfed in its presence, my brain was stunned by the thought that not just Saturn, but our entire solar system was dwarfed by the galaxy and it by the universe.

You'd think such a thought would completely kick God out of my thoughts. How could someone who made all of this have any awareness or interest in me? And yet I could feel Him watching me, showing me. Alice was showing Jack the solar system, but God was showing me His glory.

"Really, Jack? You can look at all of this and still not believe in God?"

Jack rolled his eyes. "I don't know, Hud. Can't we just enjoy this without getting all mumbo-jumbo about it?"

No, right now I couldn't. "Just tell me this, does all of this look like an accident to you?"

His head swiveled, taking in the distant sun, the close planet, and her rioting disks.

"Well, if God made all this, don't you think he'd put in a lot more stuff? Considering the distances we're looking at, even with the planets and asteroids and stuff, the solar system is pretty empty."

I started to answer and then stopped. I didn't know. In the few other times when we got into these kinds of discussions, I'd just answer without thinking, probably badly.

"I never thought of it that way, Jack. I dunno."

Jack shrugged. "We shoulda brought a camera."

"Alice," I said. "Anything we can see on the way back home?"

"Already?"

"It's getting late, Jack."

"Buzz kill, dude."

"Somebody's got to be the grownup."

"Uber buzz kill."

Alice hadn't bothered to answer with either thumb, she just took off. The sun, which had been a tiny flaming ball from Saturn, grew steadily. We were arcing around it, though I'm not sure how I knew that.

TO THE MOON, ALICE!

We passed through the asteroid field with the same gut-wrenching maneuvers and emerged to a red-ish smear in the distance that slowly and then more quickly resolved into a dirt-red ball. Mars.

While the gas giants had filled me with awe, Mars overwhelmed me with sadness, and I didn't know why.

The face of the red planet was streaked and pock-marked. For all the worn features on its surface, Mars looked like a dead world.

"Alice," I asked. "Has there ever been life here?"

Two thumbs up.

"Intelligent life?"

Alice took longer to answer than normal. Was she scanning the planet for signs of intelligence? Finally, crossed thumbs indicated she didn't know.

I felt the same way I did when I saw a homeless person, or Jack's dad when he was passed out in the yard when I came to visit. There was something wasted about Mars.

"Wanna go down and play?"

I shook my head.

"Man, what is with you, Hud? You're moody as a girl."

"You don't feel anything?"

"Annoyed."

"I think there was intelligent life here, Jack. I don't think they made it."

"Why? Alice doesn't know."

I shrugged. "Just a feeling."

"You're bumming me out, dude."

"Me too."

"Take us home, Alice," Jack said.

I couldn't take my eyes off Mars as it dwindled into a pinpoint.

Turning to where we were headed, Earth wasn't even a pinpoint of light. I scanned the space in front of us and couldn't see a thing except the sun growing in greater and greater size.

We were almost upon the Earth before we saw it. Of course. Earth was between us and the Sun, so all of Earth we could see was in shadow, which is to say, we could see nothing at all. As we got closer, artificial light rashed the night side, and I felt my spirits climb.

Rolling around the terminator, the colors of life sprang into view. Clouds wisped over blue seas and greenery hugged the brown landmasses.

The sense of God sprang brightly into my soul again and I looked over at Jack. His eyes were as wide as mine, but there seemed to be an edge to his expression.

Vertigo spun our senses as Alice plunged into the atmosphere, through clouds and the Earth swelling up as if to swat us from the sky. I closed my eyes as Jack whooped. He was a far better astronaut that I ever would be.

Closer to the ground, Alice moved so fast everything blurred around us and suddenly we dropped through the hole in Jack's dilapidated barn roof.

I stepped off on watery legs while Jack sprang down.

"Tomorrow let's stay on Earth and go to Hawaii!"

"Jack, I think I need to tell my Mom and Dad about Alice."

Jack's face shut down. "No way. We agreed, no parents."

"I don't like lying to them, Jack! It's not right!"

"Neither is breaking your promise to me. They'd take Alice away, Hud! Do you want that?"

"No! I just don't want to lie to them anymore."

"You're not lying, Hud. You're just not telling them. They wouldn't believe you, anyway."

"I'd just show them Alice, Jack."

"You can't. I've ordered Alice to run if anyone other than you or me gets near."

"You can't do that!"

"I already did."

"Is that true, Alice?"

Two thumbs up.

"I can just order her she has to, Jack."

"Nope. I told her we have to agree to change that order. And I don't."

"You did?"

"I said it, didn't I?"

I thought about that for a second. "You knew I'd want to do that?"

"Yeah. Heck, I want to do that. Your parents, not my dad," he said with some bitterness. "Your parents might not even tell, Hud, but they'd say you can't go with me."

"No duh. It's dangerous. Even you have to see that."

"So what? School is dangerous; think we should quit that?"

"No."

"Yeah, well, I might. With Alice, what do we need school for?"

"To learn?"

Jack repeated the cadence of our government teacher. "You have to learn to get a job and make your way in the world. Well, Hud, Alice is our ticket to making it in this and any other world!"

"How to do you figure?"

"Seriously, Hud? How do I figure?" He mopped the hair from his eyes, I think, to keep it from catching on fire. His eyes burned with almost fever heat. "We wanted to explore? Now we can! We can go anywhere, Hud!

Other countries, other worlds... Hey, Alice! Can we go underwater?"

Two thumbs up.

Jack hooted! "Yeah, baby! Swim with whales and sharks and giant octopuses!"

"It's squid, not octopuses. Giant squid." My voice was reedy. I didn't like where this was going at all. I hadn't seen Jack like this before. He could be intense, sure, but there was something else going on. Like a poor kid who was suddenly given the world. Not "like;" it is that. Jack didn't have anything, never seemed to want anything, but now he wanted something I wasn't sure was all that good.

Jack was just winding up. "We can go to other planets where diamonds just lay on the ground, where trees are made out of gold. We might find things scientists haven't discovered yet!"

"Promise me you'll keep going to school, Jack. Please."

He deflated. "You hate school, Hud, just as much as me!"

"Everybody hates school, but we still need to go! What if Alice breaks or something?

Jack's eyes narrowed. "Nothing's going to break Alice, Hud. Nothing and nobody."

"I'm not going to break her, Jack, but what if... what if we get hit by a silver meteor or something?"

"Then we'd be dead, too."

"Okay, okay, then somebody sees us and the FBI tracks us down. You need a fallback. School can give you that."

I watched the gears grind in his mind. It took a while, but finally, he huffed.

"For now. It's not worth the headache to quit until I'm old enough."

That was two years from now. Great, one more thing to worry about.

"I have to go home."

"So go already."

"Don't be mad, Jack."

"Don't tell me how to be, Hud."

We let that hang in the air for a while. Jack and I had never argued before. Little stuff, but he'd normally talk me into whatever we disagreed on. I'd never won before and I wasn't sure I had now.

"Hawaii tomorrow after school," I offered.

Jack shrugged and wouldn't look at me.

"I'll bring the sunblock."

Jack snorted with some humor. He finally looked at me from under his bangs.

It had to be enough.

"See you, Jack, see you, Alice."

Jack didn't say anything else and Alice couldn't.

TO THE MOON, ALICE!

I wanted to sulk all the way home. The sun had gone down, which meant it was really late again. I'd be in trouble when I got home. Again.

A Kentucky evening can break any bad mood, though. Fireflies came out to dance in the air, lighting up and winking out then back up again. It was like fairy dust. All our pre-summer nights held heat well into the late hours and crickets chirped the temperature in fast tempos. Bull frogs bleated around me. I stuck to the side of the road with tall grass in the fields. Feral cats or possums, or hopefully equally benign animals, rustled through the grass. An owl hooted.

Jack's question about the emptiness of the solar system came back to me, as well as my lack of an answer, yet here I was skipping along, surrounded by crowds of life. The awe I'd felt over Jupiter and Saturn rushed back, but in the opposite way. There I'd been overwhelmed by the vastness of it all; now I was practically swooning at the minutia around me. There were probably hundreds or thousands of little furred and feathered bodies within this square mile, yet swarming on my hand were millions of microscopic life forms. Bacteria, germs, viruses, mold, mildew, single-celled and many-celled critters... hopefully not all on my hand... All this littleness had a vastness of its own and was equally amazing as gas giants. Maybe even more so.

A car swished by—a machine of thousands of parts, heard by me, a machine of millions of parts.

The darkness seemed to squeeze in on me, but not in a threatening way. More like a hug.

"Hey, God?..."

I trailed off, not because I was expecting an answer, but because I wasn't sure what to say. Words were tiny things next to moons.

"...I get it now. Sort of. I mean, not at all, really. I don't understand but I get it. What you were showing me? All this... it's yours. I'm yours. Jack is yours, even if he doesn't know it. I guess Alice is yours, too, so you must have a reason to give her to us, right? Is it okay if I don't tell my parents? I mean, as long as you know.... But you know everything, so that doesn't count... I guess what I'm trying to say, Lord, is I can't tell my parents, but I don't want that to change things with us, either. Is that possible? What if... what if I promise to tell them if something bad happens? Is that okay?"

I was in my neighborhood now. Each of the homes glowed with the light of family, and again I was reminded that I had one and Jack didn't.

"Please take care of Jack, Lord. Let this be a good thing for him."

As I walked up our driveway, I suspected it wouldn't be. Who did that conviction come from? Me or God?

When I walked in, I expected fireworks, and it looked like I was going to be right. Mom and Dad were sitting on the couch waiting for me. Normally, they'd be in the dining room/kitchen. The couch was reserved for TV, which we rarely watched, and family meetings, where I was the only one without a vote. We hadn't had one since Ela was born, so now there were two with no vote. Didn't seem fair.

I kicked my shoes into the coat closet and walked over, taking my place on the hot seat, which is how I thought of the shorter couch across from them.

Mom looked concerned rather than angry. I looked at Dad. More concern. I got scared for a moment and looked around for Ela. She was swaddled in the laundry basket. Phew! Ela was so small I sometimes worried about her fragility.

"Hudson, we want to talk to you," Mom said.

No duh, but I wasn't about to say that.

"You're late, Sport, again," my Dad said. "That's been happening a lot lately."

I was about to protest that it was only yesterday and today, but realized I had been getting home later and later for months.

"We think we know why," my Mom said.

News to me. Except for Alice, I had no idea.

"It's Jack, isn't it?" she said.

"Let the boy speak, Janet."

I looked between them, trying not to panic. What was I supposed to say? I shrugged instead. "Jack's okay."

"I don't think he is, dear. And anyway, I was talking about his father, Jack Sr."

"Big Jack."

"Big Jack. We were friends, you know. Well, Jack's mom and I were. Big Jack was nice enough. A little rough and tumble even then..." She saw my alarm. "I mean... masculine..."

Dad's head swiveled to look at her. "Does that mean I'm not masculine, Janet?"

She closed her eyes. "You know what I mean, Tim, he was a man's man... not that you're not..."

"Macho," Dad supplied.

"Yes, macho," Mom agreed.

"Isn't that a cheese?" I said.

Dad smiled. "That's nachos, Sport. Macho means..."

"Rough and tumble," I said.

"Yeah. Not like me, gentle and urbane," Dad said.

"Nerdy."

Mom tried not to laugh. Dad sighed.

"Let's just say we were of different worlds, but tried to find common ground for the sake of our wives."

"What's that got to do with Jack? My Jack?"

"We're concerned, Hudson. Big Jack took Mandy's death hard and he... you know..."

"Drinks like a fish?" I asked.

"Yes. Just like that," Mom said.

"A big fish," Dad said.

Mom looked distressed. "We've been praying about what to do about that for the last year or so. I don't want to take Little Jack away from him because I just don't know what that would do to him. On the other hand, we've been negligent because he's a danger to Little Jack."

"Hudson," Dad said. "Does Big Jack hit Little Jack?"

"Little Jack will hit you if he hears you call him Little Jack, Dad."

"That's not an answer, son."

I thought about it. Jack had never said anything. He often had bruises, but he got into a fight almost every day with someone, so it didn't have to be from Big Jack.

"I don't know," I said truthfully.

Dad got up and paced. Mom plucked Ela from the laundry and held her close. Ela drooled. I sat.

"There are several options, Hudson," Dad said, still pacing. "We could do nothing and hate ourselves forever if anything happened to Jack. We could call the state and have Child Protective Services investigate him. Jack would likely be taken away and put into a foster home."

"Don't do that."

Dad stopped and looked at me. "Or your mother could go talk to Big Jack."

"Me?!" Mom yelled.

"Okay, me," Dad said. "I could go talk to him."

"I don't think that would go well, Dad."

"We can't let this go on, Hud."

"We're willing to take him in, Hudson, just so you know. We aren't talking about abandoning your friend," Mom said.

I thought about Alice and how both of us living here would work out. Then I inwardly yelled at myself for being more concerned about Alice than I was about Jack.

"I'll talk to him," I said. "Little Jack, that is. I don't think he'd want to leave Big Jack, though."

"Kids aren't supposed to take care of their parents, Hudson."

"Not until we're old, Sport. Then feel free," Dad said.

TO THE MOON, ALICE!

"Maybe we should pray," I said.

Mom and Dad's mouths fell open.

Chapter 5

A Bully of Bullies

I found getting to sleep difficult and waking up harder, so I missed the bus, didn't have time to ride my bike to school, and Mom ended up driving me in, getting me there ahead of the bus. Go figure. First period was still fifteen minutes off, so I hiked to the safest place in the school; the courtyard.

Much to my surprise, Jack was sitting on the edge of the terrarium (a concrete pond of dirt and plants). I'd expected him to skip school just to worry me, but he was grinning ear to ear. Even his hair was swept away from his eyes. The smile worried me.

As I approached, he pointed at his wristband and raised his eyebrows. I displayed mine and his grin got bigger.

I can only blame the magnetism of that evil grin that I never saw Pruit coming. One second I was walking, the next I was running into a wall of flesh.

"Who you callin' a bully, punk!" Pruit spit down at me.

My eyes shot wide, and I peered around him to see if Jack was coming to my rescue. He sat, still smiling and wiggled his fingers at me.

"N-n-n-not me," I sputtered, too scared to see the irony of his question.

"So your buddy the psycho was lyin'? That what you're sayin', punk?"

I nodded like an idiot. How mad at me was Jack? I backed up, right into another not-bully intent on seeing me in pain.

"Tryin' to run? I don't think so!" His eyes were scanning for adults and from the glee on his face, I knew he didn't see any.

I didn't even see his fist draw back, but I did see it snap forward, straight into my gut. I folded over it in reflex.

Then realized something.

It hadn't hurt.

I stood up. Nope, no pain.

Pruit squinted at me and threw a fist at my jaw. I tried to flinch away, but not fast enough. His fist skidded off. When he tried to break my nose, his fist stopped short of my face. The shock of the surprise stop shuddered up his arm, and he squeaked.

He couldn't hurt me!

"Did you just squeak, Pruit?" Jack said, joining us.

Pruit tried to shove him away. Jack didn't budge.

"Hits like a girl, doesn't he, Hud?"

Pruit's face turned darker red and his eyes darted like fish. He reared back with all his strength for the hardest punch of his life. I wondered if he'd break his fist.

"MR. PRUIT!" came a deep voice. Mr. Jeeries shouldered through the knot of people drawn to watch.

Pruit thought about it. I could see it on his face. Land the punch and be expelled...?

His breath shuddered out like a dieseling truck. He dropped his arm and tried to stalk off, but a large, black hand clapped on his shoulder.

Mr. Jeeries was so cool, I liked him even though he was a P.E. teacher and lived in a nylon sweat suit burning the school's colors.

"You all right, Mr. Cook?" he said in those Darth Vader tones.

I nodded happily.

"He hits like a girl, Mr. Jeeries," Jack trumpeted.

"Never met my sister, have you, Mr. Taylor?" Jeeries said.

"Nope."

"Be glad you haven't." His shovel-sized hand dug deeper into Pruit's shoulder, enough to make the bigger boy wince. "Why don't we head over to the principal's office and go over the reason why we don't hit kids smaller than ourselves, shall we, Mr. Pruit? I presume why we don't hit bigger kids speaks for itself?"

No one had first names in Mr. Jeeries' world.

Jack and I snuck off in the other direction as everyone watched Pruit do the perp-walk to the admin building. Some of them cheered.

I grabbed Jack's arm and was a little surprised I could. Our force fields knew the difference between touch and violence.

"You knew?" I said.

"That's how much I forgive you for being a jerk, Hud. I figured it out last night when—I mean at the barn, you know? When I jumped off the rafter? Anyway, the first thing I wanted to do was find Pruit and have a real knock-down-drag-out with him being the one knocked down and dragged out, but nooooo! I let you have all the fun."

"No, it would have been fun if I'd known he couldn't hurt me."

"So now you know!"

My mind swirled. "How can we use this?"

"Rob banks," Jack said.

I frowned at him.

"Not now, not now," he said. "Only as a last resort!"

"Jack!"

"You're such a girl."

Evangalina was walking our way and caught that last remark. She planted herself in front of us with a hand on her hip and flared eyes. "You just stop right there, Hudson Cook! Why is that an insult?" she said with all the fire she threw at everything.

"I didn't say it!" I said.

"You're offended by it!" she said, her head thrown back.

"No guy wants to be a girl," I said.

"No regular guy," said Jack.

"I ain't talking to you, weed," Evangalina said to Jack. Back to me. "I am tired of that lame put down. Hit like a girl, throw like a girl, you ARE a girl! I LIKE bein' a girl, and you know what else?" she said, her index finger weaving like a snake in front of my face, "YOU like me bein' a girl!"

Jack kicked me. "Stop blushing. You're embarrassing me."

Evangelina has a thing for me. I don't know why, but she does and she can turn me into an idiot just by looking at me.

"So, then, you don't want him to be a girl then, either, right?" Jack crowed at her.

"Get me some weed-be-gone and that's the end of you, boy," Evangalina said, her cobra finger pointing him away. "Hudson's walkin' me to class!"

She wrapped her arm around mine with no protest from my force field. Betrayed by Alice.

"I ain't no weed," Jack said.

Word cycled through school at light speed. Pruit was expelled and without him as the gang leader, the minor bullies would back off. The final weeks of school would be a breeze! Then we got to Spanish class.

Miss Bangler was wearing a moo-moo the size of a Coleman tent that was the color of rainbows. That meant two things. Our hefty teacher was in a good mood, and in a lazy mood. The poster-teacher for manic-depression, Miss Bangler went from literal dark lows to blinding highs. Only she got the productivity side of the illness all wrong. When she was depressed, she worked like a fiend, doling out misery to match her own. Swinging high, though, and she didn't want to do anything but beam. The brighter the colors she wore, the higher and lazier she'd be. That meant no lesson plans, no assignments, not even homework.

"POP-QUIZ DAY!" she hollered, her arms spread out like wings. "Take out a piece of paper and pen and put everything else on the floor. I am going to SPEAK and YOU are going to translate! I might even sing!"

We groaned in response. Jack crossed his eyes. We all reached for paper. Happy or sad, we were the ones who paid.

"Don't you cross your eyes at me, Jack Taylor, they might freeze that way!" Miss Bangler said. A tingle raced through my arm.

"If they did, could I go to the nurse?" Jack said. Kids swiveled to look at him.

"Is that what you want, Mr. Jack?" she said, "to go to the nurse, rather than to stay in my class and have a wonderful time with all of us?"

"It isn't a wonderful time, and none of us are having fun, Miss Bangler!"

"I am!" she trumpeted.

"You would," he said.

Miss Bangler applauded while the kids raised their eyebrows at Jack.

"What!" he said.

"Since when do you understand Spanish?" asked Juan. Jack hadn't learned any the whole year.

"I don't," Jack said with venom.

"Coulda fooled me," Juan said. "I barely understood what she was saying."

Miss Bangler was still clapping. "You've been sandbagging, Jack! I'm so proud of you!"

"For what? Who's sandbagging?" he said.

"See?" said Juan. "I didn't know that meant sandbagging. I don't even know what sandbagging is in English."

The kids were stirring, and my arm was still tingling. I think I understood.

"Jack," I whispered at him.

"What?"

"Is your arm tingling?" I whispered.

"Yeah." He wasn't whispering.

I took a different approach. "Miss Bangler, that was flawless Spanish!" I said.

"She wasn't speaking Spanish, moron!"

"Yes," I hissed at him, "she was!"

Miss Bangler lit up even brighter. She applauded even faster. "Jacccccck! You're THINKING IN SPANISH!" she screamed.

No, he wasn't. I turned so she couldn't see my face and only Jack could. "The wristbands are translating!" I whispered.

"Huh?"

"I think we're all ready for the test now, Miss Bangler!" I said.

She looked at Jack with a maniacal grin. "You're going to do well, Jack. I can feel it!"

Jack crossed his eyes at me.

Whispering again, "Just write down what you hear, whether it's in English or Spanish!"

Miss Bangler was singing now, and we were all writing furiously. Jack and I heard her clearly in English, everyone else in Spanish. Even so, it was difficult to keep up. Around me, pens were being slapped down as kids gave up.

Peeking at Jack, he wasn't writing at all. He stared at Miss Bangler with his mouth open.

When the bell rang, we flooded out the door. Juan sighed beside us. "Figures. She finally does something I can probably pass and she'll never grade it."

True, that. At one of her highs, Miss Bangler couldn't be bothered to grade the tests. We'd all get As because she'd feel too good to actually think about it.

Are all schools this weird?

Jack was pulling me away from the crowd.

"What was that? What happened?"

"You know that tingling? I think Alice, or the wristbands or whatever, was translating for us. The tingling was bone conduction!"

"What's that?"

"It means we were hearing with our bones, not ears, so no one else could hear it but us."

"Freaky."

"But cool."

"Way cool."

We shoulda brought shorts.

Alice was tucked away in the... what was that? Jungle? Woods? Whatever, all the fronds and palms that backed the beach were.

We'd told Alice to take us to Hawaii, and we rocketed into space again, which was not what either of us expected. Once the panic faded and we were looking at Earth rotating beneath us, I wondered if there was a planet named Hawaii Alice was taking us to. Then Alice plunged back down and it looked like we were aiming for the ocean, but then a series of ragged dots became islands. Alice picked a smaller one and shot into whatever that was called with the freaky trees and stuff.

She knew enough to stay out of sight from other people, I guess. Even the beach we were running around on was almost empty. I didn't know Hawaii had any empty beaches. The only others on the beach were tiny brown kids, maybe 3 or 4 years old. There were some brown old men further down with fishing poles, but no one our age or even a little older.

"They must all be in school," I'd ventured.

"School's not out over here?" Jack asked.

I looked at the sun almost straight overhead. "It's earlier here, I think."

We'd rolled up our pants as high as they could go and splashed around in the surf. The water was wonderfully warm and minnows darted around our feet.

Jack looked around and said, "to heck with it," and started pulling off his clothes.

"Jack!"

"Look at them!" he said, waving at the kids. "They're naked!"

"They're babies!"

He shaded his eyes and looked down at the beach. "Think the old guys are starkers, too."

"Ew!"

"I'm leaving my underwear on, okay?" He threw his pants onto the beach and plunged into the water and immediately came back up. "Blech! Water tastes awful!"

I looked at my wristband.

TO THE MOON, ALICE!

"Hey, Alice," I said into my wrist. "Can you turn on the force field so no water gets in?"

A faint tingle spread over my body, and I grinned. I jumped into the water, clothes, glasses and all, and went under.

No wetness. Warm, but not wet. I opened my eyes. The water was too shallow to get a really good idea of the new world around me, so I went back up. "Come on!" I yelled.

We pounded out to sea, the water barely up to our knees. Jack left his clothes on the beach, his dirty briefs dripping inside his force field. We had to run for a while, but finally we hit deeper water, plunging beneath the waves.

It was beautiful! The sandy sea floor sloped away and bigger fish seemed to soar around us! From down here, the surface of the ocean looked like an undulating roof.

Then I realized how deep it was. The surface was a long way up there! I flailed violently as my lungs strained. Panic hit me hard; I couldn't seem to climb!

I felt sudden pressure on my stomach, emptying the little air I had left from my lungs. Reflexively I drew a breath even as my brain screamed not to!

And my lungs filled. With air, not water. I breathed rapidly. Plenty of air.

Looking around, I saw Jack struggling, the compression of his gut and the calming realization that he could breathe. Under! Water!

I started laughing, and so did Jack. I could hear him clearly.

"That was scary!" Jack said.

"Terrifying!" I agreed.

"Cool!"

"Awesome!"

A giant shadow passed over us. I wet my pants.

"It's a turtle!" shouted Jack.

It was! Not a shark, a sea turtle. I wet my pants for nothing. Maybe Jack wouldn't notice.

"Do you think our force fields could stop a shark?" I said.

"Dunno."

"Let's not find out."

I swam down and examined some coral. All around us, odd-shaped life scuttled and flitted through the crystal water. Jack thrashed from one place to another, touching anything he could get near. I was content to watch them without interfering.

A school of colorful fish burst from behind the lumpy outcrop and Jack raised a hand at them and squinted.

"Jack, what are you doing?"

"Shhhh. I'm talking to them."

"Your lips aren't moving."

He thrashed around. "I'm thinking at them, okay?"

"Didn't know you had it in you, Jack."

"Ha-ha. Dude, we have super powers! I was trying to figure out if we're like Aquaman or the Sub-Mariner." He pronounced it, sub-mareener. I didn't correct him as he went back to thinking at the fish. They serenely swam away.

"Not Aquaman, then," he said. Upon reflection, "'S'okay, though. Aquaman's lame."

"Sub-Mariner can't talk to fish?" I asked.

"I dunno, but he's got pointy ears. That's pretty cool."

Jack logic. Okay.

"Wouldn't we be more like Iron Man, only instead of a metal suit we have force fields?" I said.

"Can Iron Man go underwater?"

I shrugged, which felt weird surrounded by water, and sent me upward a little bit. "He can do anything the writers want him to do, I guess."

"Hey, he can shoot energy out of his hands! Think we can do that?" Before I could answer, he threw his hand out, palm up toward me, and strained. I ducked, but nothing happened anyway.

"Huh-oh," Jack said, looking past me.

I thrashed around. Brown arms and legs pinwheeled in from the surface, bubbles frothing around them. Dull thrumming hit our ears. An old man dove down from above a dozen yards off and looked around. When he saw us, his eyes went wide, and he resurfaced. He must have pointed everyone toward us because now the arms and legs were coming toward us.

Each pair of arms suddenly became men as they dove down, and five naked men wove into the water looking at us. One finally pointed to the surface, and we all swam up there. Breaking the surface was like entering a different world, much brighter and harsher than below.

"Thought you were dead," said one old man.

"Et by a shark," said another.

"Nope! We're fine," Jack said brightly.

The men stared at us.

"How is that?" asked the first man. "Is it those things?" he said, pointing at Jack's wristband. It was a good guess, seeing as it wouldn't be his underwear, the only other thing Jack was wearing.

"We're submarine people from the Atlantic!" Jack said.

"Pacific," I said.

"Yeah, Pacific."

The men looked at each other. "Why you speaking English, then?"

"Are you speaking English?" Jack asked. Like me, he must have assumed their own language was being translated by the bands.

One more round of staring and the first fellow smiled with blinding white teeth. "You guys are weird!"

He headed back toward shore and waved us to follow. Jack shrugged at me and started thrashing his way in. The water was warm, but the air was blistering. We were much slower than the men, who were all sitting on the beach when we slogged ashore.

Other than self-inflicted moisture, I was dry when we came up.

The old man grinned. "Is that the newest thing from Apple?"

"You know about Apple?" Jack said.

"Hey, kid, we're Americans just like you." He was a large man, thick in the body with a broad, happy face.

"Americans wear clothes," Jack said.

"Looks who's talking, fella. Name's Ken. What's yours?" Ken shot back.

I elbowed Jack before he could answer. "Uh, I'm Joe, and this here's Mike," I said.

"Where can I get one of those, 'Joe?'"

I fidgeted. "You can't, Ken. One of a kind, sorry."

"Maybe we'll take those, then," said the youngest of the old guys.

Jack bristled, fists rising. "Bring it on, buddy!"

Ken waved off his friend. "Nobody's taking anything, Bob!" he growled. Softening again, "but what about buying? Got a nice boat I'll trade."

"No thanks, sir," I said.

"Got a nice daughter," Ken said.

"How nice?" asked Jack. I rolled my eyes.

"We'll just be going now, sir," I said.

"Go ahead. Who's stopping you? Gonna swim back to Pacifica?" Ken said.

I looked around. I'd memorized where we'd put Alice and it was just a short way up the beach. We couldn't go to her while they were around.

Jack and I were on the same wavelength. He made a little hop in the air and said, "Yep! That's just what we're gonna do. Come on H... uh, Mike."

Ken pointed at me. "He's Joe. You're Mike."

"Whatever, come on, dude," he said, slapping my belly with the back of his hand and looking at me for the first time.

"Dude. You wet your pants."

"At least I have pants."

Jack looked stricken. Scanning the beach, he said, "Hey, where are my clothes?"

"Finders/keepers, kid," Bob volunteered.

"Dude!"

"Hey, I got a grandkid 'bout your age. Sometimes the ocean gives, sometimes it takes away."

Jack stalked over to Bob, his feet making sand fly. "Give 'em back!"

Bob, towering over Jack, shrugged his shoulder. "Already gone, kid. One set 'a clothes, two sets 'a shoes."

"Hey!" I said, realizing one of the pairs of shoes was mine.

"Bob," Ken piped up. "We ain't thieves."

"What thievin'? Pile a' clothes left on the beach for two hours, who's to know the owner's comin' back? Kids took 'em already."

Ken shrugged at us.

"Two hours?" That meant we'd been gone for several and it was getting late back home. Again.

Ken saw my stricken face. "Gotta be somewhere, Joe?"

"Come on guys, we have to get out of here and..." I shook my head. "We can't go until you do."

Bob grinned. "I ain't goin' anywhere."

Ken sighed. He stood up from the sand where he'd been sitting, using a small canvas bag to swat the sand from his dark skin. "Come on, Bob. Stop being a jerk."

"Thanks, Ken," I said to the mostly-grumbling men as they wandered away.

"Sure thing, kid. Oh, one more thing." He spun and snapped a picture with a small digital camera. "For Facebook." They all laughed and moved away, the burning sand having no effect on their feet. I could feel it through the force field.

When they'd finally gone far enough, we made our way to Alice, careful to look around for prying eyes.

"How am I going to explain my shoes disappearing?"

"How am I going to explain my clothes?"

I'd been to the beach before, of course, and the worst part was always getting the sand off. Force fields, where have you been all my life?

Hopping up on Alice, Jack gave her instructions. "Stay low, Alice, and take us through the jungle cover for as long as you can. Those guys will be looking for something weird."

Even as best friends, I don't normally see Jack starkers. Until now, seeing him on the platform, I hadn't realized how skinny he'd gotten as if he hadn't been eating for a long time. It brought to mind what my parents had talked about. As we zoomed through the jungle, weaving around trees, something else occurred to me.

"Jack? How did you find out the force fields prevented us from getting hurt?"

Normally, he'd wipe the hair from his eyes and answer without thinking. This time, his hair hung over his eyes as he took his time.

"Told you. The rafter."

Before I could say anything else, Alice shot into the air. "Hey, Alice! A little warning next time!"

As the island state receded from sight below us, I wondered how many photos were being taken, or were we moving too fast? Would we be in the news again, or just Facebook?

Alice returned us to Jack's barn and before we could talk, he slunk off through the tall grass toward home.

Luckily, my pants had dried out in the Hawaiian heat, but walking home with bare feet was going to be a challenge.

And then it wasn't. I love force fields!

CHAPTER 6

The Invitation

I WAS GROUNDED. MY parents were asserting their authority to expect me home at a given time, which I had failed to do since we found Alice.

My parents aren't heartless, though. Their concern for Jack's well-being meant that I couldn't go out, but if Jack wanted to come over, he could.

I had to wait until Wednesday to tell him, though, because he skipped school on Tuesday. I stressed all day, didn't learn a thing, offended Evangalina by ignoring her (which I always do, but normally while blushing furiously), and thrilled Miss Bangler by answering all her direct questions without realizing she'd said them in Spanish. Mostly, I worried over the question of how to check up on Jack. They had a telephone, but it wasn't always in service, like now, and I couldn't go looking for him after school.

I almost decided to skip my last couple classes and use the time to track down Jack, but a surprise assembly prevented that. Half the school attended fifth period and the other half sixth period. I was in the first half, but knew any hope of skipping afterward would be foiled by hyper-vigilant teachers on the watch for class-cutters.

The assembly was to watch a motivational speaker with a message about bullying and self-esteem accompanied by funny stories and really loud music. Normally I would have loved it, and had even seen this guy at a church rally once, but today the music just gave me a headache. Jack would have loved this. The speaker was a former wrestler, former partier, and great storyteller. His message was spot-on for Jack in so many ways that every time I tried to listen, I just got more worried about Jack.

If I walked home, I could swing by Jack's house. But that would take too long and Mom would know. Then inspiration struck. I could tell Mom the truth! Jack hadn't shown up, and I was worried. Could I go check on him and come right back home?

I hadn't seen the flaw in logic. Mom said she'd drive me over herself, and no amount of argument could dissuade her.

With Ela strapped in her car seat, we drove off, me giving directions.

I strained to see over the tall grass as we entered their dirt driveway. Please don't let Big Jack be home, please don't let Big Jack be home...

Of course, Big Jack was home. He was sitting on the dilapidated porch swing, shoulders rounded, with a beer can in his hand and five more in a plastic holder dangling from his free hand.

I held onto Mom's sleeve when she tried to get out, but she just untangled my fingers and stepped out with a smile.

"Afternoon, Jack," she called, picking her way to the porch.

Big Jack peered at her and cocked his head. "Janet?"

"You remember!"

"'Course I do. This is only my first," he said, tipping his beer to her.

"Hudson was worried about Little Jack."

"What for?"

"He didn't go to school today."

Big Jack's eyes narrowed. "Today's a teacher's day or something, Jackie said." He sounded like a threatening storm.

Mom snapped her fingers. "Well, there you go, Hudson. Little Jack was in the half of the class that was off today. I told you it went by last name and not first." She turned back to Big Jack. "I don't know why they don't do the whole school at once. Make things a lot easier. Is he here, Jack? Hudson would like to see him."

Big Jack leaned back and chose to accept the lie. I didn't know Mom had it in her. He waved the ring of beer cans toward the barn. "He's been pokin' around out there all day. You know the way, Hud."

"Yes, sir." I didn't know he knew my name.

"You go on and see your friend, Hudson, while Jack and I have a talk," Mom said, smiling easily.

I shook my head tightly. She winked at me and shooed me away. I obeyed, reluctantly.

"It's been a long time, Jack."

Big Jack studied the porch. "Everything's been a long time, Janet. Have a beer?"

I was just getting out of earshot when Mom floored me. "Don't mind if I do, Jack."

Mom drinking a beer? I shoved through the last of the tall grass and pushed open the barn door.

It was empty. No Jack. No Alice.

Trudging back to the porch, anger and concern dueling like fighter planes in my head, I saw Mom sitting on the top step of the dirty porch, her legs primly tucked beside her. She held her beer gently in one hand and gazed at Big Jack without judgment. Dandelion fluff drifted in the warm breeze, chased by gnats in the golden sun. I realized with a flash of maturity that this would be a beautiful picture.

Big Jack still stared at the floor. An empty can stood sentry on the arm rail while another stood duty in his hand, the ring of beers now cut down to three.

"...fine boy, Jack. He's kind and protective. I hope you're as proud of your little man as I am."

Big Jack nodded his head but said nothing.

"Well! Hudson! Did you find Little Jack?"

"Um, yeah. Sure. I told him I was grounded and all. He'll come over when he feels like it." I said.

"Well, good then." She rose gracefully and patted Big Jack's knee. "It was good to see you, Jack. You both need to come to dinner sometime," she said.

"Sure, sure," he mumbled.

"When?" Mom said.

"Huh?"

"When would you like to come over?"

Big Jack blinked.

"Uh, well you know..."

"How about Friday? I'll put on a nice spread and you and Little Jack can come over. Oh, it will be a wonderful time! I'll take care of everything, you just bring yourself and Jack! Don't forget now! In fact, I'll send Hudson over to remind you!"

"Um, Janet, I don't think Friday…"

"Yes. Friday, Jack. You'll be there." The steel in her voice was gentle, but undeniable.

We climbed into the car with Big Jack's mouth still hanging open.

"Hold this for me, would you, Hudson?" She handed me her beer that was open but untouched.

Ela was still asleep, and Mom waved as we backed out and drove away. Big Jack looked very small.

I sniffed the beer and flinched at the sharp smell.

"That went well!" Mom said.

"Think they'll really come?"

"You'll make sure they will, Hudson."

I thought about making Big Jack do anything he didn't want to do. The beer felt big in my hand.

"Can I have a sip?" I asked.

"Sure," Mom said, full of surprises today.

"Really?"

She nodded, eyes twinkling.

I sipped.

And gagged.

"Nasty, isn't it?"

"If you don't like it, why'd you ask for it?"

"Oh, I like it."

"You do?"

"Yep. And I'll finish it when we get home. Meanwhile, there's one less for Big Jack to drink."

I'd have to file this away. Mom can be sneaky...

Chapter 7

School is Crazy

I SAT IN MY room, glowering at the poster of the solar system on my wall. Where was Jack? Had he gone off to the dinosaur planet? Had he been eaten?

I plucked at the wristband absently. Then I wanted to smack myself! The wristband! How stupid could I be? Lifting it to my mouth, I hissed, "Jack? Jack, you there?"

"Hang on," came a whispered reply. "I gotta sneak out."

I could imagine him slinking past Big Jack and his can of beer. My foot tapped as I waited.

"Don't be mad," came the disembodied voice.

"Why would I be mad, Jack? Because you skipped school? Because you took off with Alice when we said we had to go together? Or maybe because you've been giving Alice orders behind my back?"

"Yeah, for all those things," Jack said.

My eyes narrowed. Was he making fun of me? "I wish I could see your face, Jack!"

A wart bubbled up on the wristband and a blue beam stabbed out, painting Jack's face in blue light.

"Whoa!" I said, in concert with Jack's miniature face. He must have been seeing me, too. "That's way cool!" blue Jack said. And it was. I felt my anger fade.

"Where'd you go, Jack?"

"Oh, you know, around."

"The dinosaur planet, Jack?"

Blue Jack sighed. "Almost. I was gonna, but I felt guilty."

"Where then?"

"....Venus."

"Venus! Not Mars?"

"We saw Mars."

"Were there any girls there, Jack?"

Blue Jack pursed his lips. "No. And it wasn't particularly girlish, either. We went down to the surface and I couldn't see anything. It was all gassy. Kinda guy-like that way, if you think about it. Then Alice did this... thing. Like using her holograms to show me what was there. Lots of little volcano-things, only real small."

"Geysers?" I said.

"Yeah, I guess. And the mother of all storms, Hud, it was cool! Lightning crashed everywhere! The noise was terrible until Alice tamped it down!"

"You could have been hurt, Jack!"

"Naw, Alice had my back."

"Jack, you could have! That's why we go together. If lightning hit you and knocked you out, do you think Alice could get you back on her platform?"

"Maybe."

"Together, Jack! That's a rule!"

"All right, already! Together! I won't go into space without you again, Hud, promise!"

"How do I know you'll do it, Jack? Huh?"

"Fine!" Blue Jack's face got stormy. "Alice! You won't take either of us into outer space unless we're together! That's an order!" Blue Jack winked out and Alice did a double-thumbs up. Jack popped up again. "There! Satisfied?"

"And you'll come to school."

Blue Jacked sighed. "Okay, I'll come to school. Happy?"

"Yes!"

"Good! Jack out!"

"Hud out!"

The blue face disappeared.

I forgot to tell him about Friday. Oops.

I missed the bus again, and Mom refused to take me, so I'd "learn my lesson." That meant running to school if I wanted to catch Jack before first period. Out of breath and panting like a dog, I all but tumbled down the hill to the back gate of school. It was on the far side of the football field, which would have given me pause before I had a force field. No telling who would be hanging out back there. The field was fenced with a gap where the gate was supposed to be.

I expected smoking seniors; what I got was Evangalina. No idea why she was there, but that didn't stop her from blocking the gate, so I couldn't get past.

"Hey there, Hudson," she said with that musical quality that usually flamed my cheeks. Not this time, I had places to be.

"Let me by, Evangalina."

Wrong tone. She scowled and balled her fists on her hips. "You ain't got no account to talk to me that way!"

"Sorry, can I get by? I need to find Jack."

"The weed ain't here," she said, unmoving.

That surprised me. "He said he'd come today." Jack wasn't one to lie. I had to call him on the wristband, but not in front of Evangalina. Could I vault the fence?

The squint of her eyes said that would be a bad idea.

"Hud? You there?" chirped my wristband. Jack!

TO THE MOON, ALICE!

Evangelina's scowl deepened. "What was that?" Her head weaved back and forth, looking for Jack behind me. She didn't move, though, intent on blocking my path.

I did the only thing I could think of. While she craned left to see beyond me, I lunged in, but instead of kissing her cheek, she turned and it was lips I hit with mine!

She stepped back, a weird look of happiness and surprise on her face. Mine was on fire and my lips burned with extra heat. I darted past her as she lifted stunned fingers to her mouth, moving in a dreamy, slow motion.

What had I done?

Jack called out again as I ran across the field, eyes darting to see if anyone had witnessed my stupidity.

"No face, Alice! Jack, where are you?" I said into my wrist.

"I'll be there, Hud, I'm just... running late is all."

"Why?"

"It's just a thing, Hud. Catch you at lunch! Bye!"

"Jack!"

I stole a look back. Evangalina hadn't moved from the gate. She just watched me, swaying side to side.

What had I done?

My morning classes were excruciating. I now had first-hand knowledge of Einstein's Relativity Theory and it didn't seem to work in space. Alice approached light-speed without ill effect, but school experienced time dilation like crazy. Normally, I read my textbooks during class. I can learn twice as much with a book as I can by a teacher droning on, but today I was too distracted to read. Ms. Simms, a teacher who was deeply suspicious of me to begin with because I paid no attention in class but aced all the tests, noticed I wasn't reading and mistook it for awareness.

"Mr. Cook, you've chosen to join us today?" At least, I guess that's what she said. I didn't hear it, but everyone was staring at me. At first I thought they knew about me and Evangalina, but figured it out when Ms. Simms sighed and said, "I guess not," and resumed the class.

I went back to worrying about Jack until the kid behind me kicked my chair. Ms. Simms was looking over her glasses at me again.

"Ma'am?"

"What class is this, Mr. Cook?"

My brain went into search mode but didn't come up with much. "Some kind of English class, isn't it?"

A hand shot up in the front row. "It's Language Sciences, Ms. Simms."

Ms. Simms shot her a curdling look. "I was speaking to Mr. Cook, Miss Standish."

TO THE MOON, ALICE!

Cindy—Miss Standish—pouted as if her 4.0 was being threatened.

"That's like English, isn't it, Ms. Simms?" I said.

She spun on her flats and announced to the class: "Students, Mr. Cook clearly isn't interested in my teaching. Are any of you?"

Cindy's hand shot up. Everyone else looked confused. They knew a trick question when they heard one.

"It seems you're not alone, Mr. Cook."

"Cindy likes it, Ms. Simms."

"Miss Standish is a suck-up, Mr. Cook. Perhaps you'd like to teach class."

Cindy glared at me as if I had said it.

"I'm sure you'd do much better than me, Ms. Simms."

"Nonsense, Mr. Cook. The subject is the Dewey Decimal System. Go."

Ms. Simms is one of those super-skinny older women who at one time were allowed to hit kids, you could just tell. A rap with those boney knuckles would hurt, even through my force field.

I opened my mouth...

"In front of the class, Mr. Cook."

Swiveling out of my seat, I stood up and noticed for the first time I was taller than Ms. Simms. Weird what you notice when you're in trouble.

From the front of the class, I looked at her, giving her one more chance to call it off. She nodded just once.

Two dozen pairs of eyes looked hopefully at me, hoping to see me crash and burn. I shrugged.

"The Dewey Decimal System is an archaic method for keeping track of books by category." I saw Ms. Simms flinch. I don't know if it was because of the word "archaic" or that I knew about this.

"Melvil Dewey invented it on the country's centennial, which was when, Cindy?"

Cindy perked up, "1876!"

"Right you are, Miss Sssstandish. They didn't have search engines or the Internet back then, so numbers were the best they could come up with."

The kids laughed, and Ms. Simms slid into my seat and settled back, determined to make the most of it.

"Back in the old days, libraries had paper books, a lot of them, no computers or DVDs or stuff like that," I said. Our library had books still, of course, but the stacks were ignored for the huge digital library. "Dewey's system breaks all books, even fiction, into ten categories..."

By the end of class, I'd exhausted my knowledge of Dewey's System, the Library of Congress System and given a general lesson on Man's need to classify things as a means to understand large subjects.

TO THE MOON, ALICE!

When the bell rang, the kids seemed surprised. As they poured out of their seats, Ms. Simms sidled up to me. "Perhaps you've found your calling, Mr. Cook."

My horrified look surprised her. "Middle School forever? No way!"

She just sighed in return. Teachers sighed a lot.

Lunch was over and I'd finished the Grandma's Chocolate Chip Cookie and Coke I'd traded my sandwich and juice for when Jack fell onto the bench beside me.

"You didn't answer my calls, Jack."

"Couldn't, Hud. Too many people around."

"Where were you!" I turned to him and realized he was wearing new clothes that looked expensive. I'd never seen Jack in new clothes of any kind. "Where'd you get those!"

"Store. Where do you get your clothes?"

I glanced around. "Where'd you get the money?" I hissed.

"Looks like I missed lunch. Bummer. Well, off to class!"

"Jack!"

He rotated slowly and stared through hooded eyes.

"You didn't steal it, did you? With Alice?"

"Nooo."

"Then how?"

"I sold something."

"Not Alice!"

"No! Of course not! As if, Hud!"

"What then?"

"We're gonna be late for class."

"Jack!"

"Late. For. Class." He spun on his new heels and stalked out of the lunchroom.

We wouldn't share a class for two more periods.

My heart sank. My next class was with Evangalina.

Burying myself in a textbook didn't work. Evangalina took the seat next to me and stared at me. All period. Mr. "Just call me Joe" Herbinson, who insisted we use his first name despite it being against school policy, finally noticed.

"Does Hud have something in his ear, Evangalina?"

The class broke up in laughter.

Evangalina sighed. "No, Mr. Joe."

"Then perhaps you might consider the polynomials on the board."

"That's math, Mr. Joe, and I don't do math." She kept watching me. I could feel it.

Mr. Joe was a former flower child, even though he wasn't old enough to be born before the sixties. His stringy gray hair hung thinly past his shoulder and he wore granny glasses that were so thick they always slid down his long nose. He loved math. He had a team of "mathletes" as geeky as he was who met after school to do math for fun. Mr. Joe could not compute kids who didn't love math.

"Everybody does math, Evangalina, it's the language of the universe," Mr. Joe said. It was his favorite phrase and could be a lament or a battle-cry. This was a lament.

"Mmmmmm-mmmmm, Mr. Joe. The language of the universe is love," Evangalina breathed. The class laughed, and I blushed. Mr. Joe took it as a challenge.

"That's cool, that's cool, but it's all the same thing," Mr. Joe gushed. "Class, love is math; math is love. It's the universe, man!"

This was my salvation. Mr. Joe was inches from a major league monolog, he just needed a push. I raised my hand.

"Mr. Joe?"

"Yes, Hud?"

"In the calculus of love, I'm pretty sure 1+1=3."

Mr. Joe closed his eyes, shaking his head and waving his hands, getting good and wound up.

Malissa stood up. We went to church together. "Mr. Joe, huh-unh, this is starting to sound like Sex Ed., and my parents said I'm supposed to walk out when that happens. They say school is no place for that kind of talk, no way!"

Mr. Joe's eyes snapped open, and he rushed to her, waving his hands in small circles. "No, no, no, Malissa, this is, like, transcendent! Math is everywhere, yes, in... that subject... it's true, but right here in our subject..."

"And in life!" I piped up.

"Yes!" He pointed at me.

"The Fibonacci Sequence!" I shouted in unabashed manipulation.

Mr. Joe's eyes practically rolled up in his head.

"Yessssssss!"

The rest of the period was spent with Mr. Joe reciting all the exciting and wondrous places the repeating sequence of numbers showed up. It was an impressive list, and I'd geeked out on it myself a few years ago when my youth pastor brought it up. Mr. Joe was an atheist who found God in numbers, not the Bible, and he preached his version of truth with more passion than any pastor I'd seen.

Evangalina wasn't listening, though, unless she was looking for it in the whorls of my ear.

Finally, it was Spanish. It was the first time I'd ever looked forward to that class. Naturally, Jack showed up late. I glared at him the second he walked in.

He thought about sitting somewhere other than next to me, but decided against it. Wisely. Talking was difficult, with Miss Bangler dancing around the class, checking our homework. Literally dancing. She even sang her remarks, usually in Spanish, so the kid couldn't understand her.

The desks were set wide apart to accommodate these sprightly reviews, which also made talking difficult.

I leaned way over in my seat to whisper, hoping no other kids could hear. Before I could, though, Juan spun in his seat directly in front of Jack. "Lookin' good, Bro. Things pickin' up for your dad?"

Normally, mentioning Jack's dad resulted in a fight, but not with Juan. Big as he was, Juan was what my mom called a "good soul" with no meanness in him.

"Same old, same old, man," Jack said, mildly.

One of Pruitt's friends changed all that.

"Bet he stole 'em, didn't ya, Maniac?"

To my ears, it sounded like a compliment, honestly. Pruitt's gang had a weird sense of respect. Jack, not so much. The Maniac launched himself over his desk and grabbed the boy's hair, yanking hard and getting in a punch before Juan tried to step in.

Juan, as much as me, kept Jack from going too far because Jack would never strike the big peacemaker. It's amazing to me that Jack's whirlwind was controlled enough to know who he was hitting and who he wasn't.

Typically, Juan would pick Jack up by the shirt collar or wrap him in a bear hug. This time, his hand stopped two inches from Jack's collar. Surprise registered on Juan's face even as the Pruitt wanna-be started hollering and other kids started chanting, "Fight! Fight!"

Jack landed three or four more solid punches while across the room. Miss Bangler waved her hands like birds in flight but made no other move.

Juan moved in for the bear hug, but his arms couldn't enclose him and slid off. The kid under attack threw a chair at Jack, but it bounced off. The force field made this a one-sided fight and Jack wasn't slowing down, no matter how much I shouted at him.

Kids crowded around, preventing Miss Bangler from getting into the thick of it.

Taking a deep breath, I jumped between Jack, and his target just as he threw a fist. Our force fields sparked when they came into contact and the kids shrank back. Panicked, I raised my wrist to my mouth, scrunched my face and hissed, "Alice, drop my field," just as Jack threw another roundhouse. Jack's fist crashed into my eye with no resistance and my face exploded... that's what it felt like, anyway. I slid to the floor bonelessly.

Jack immediately dropped to my side, all the fight gone from him.

"Hud! I'm sorry! Hud! You OK? I didn't mean..."

"BOTH OF YOU TO THE VICE PRINCIPAL'S OFFICE RIGHT NOW!" We all looked at her, even me, lolling my head in her direction. She was on top of a desk, moo-moo flapping, hands pin-wheeling, and in real danger of falling.

Juan broke the silence. "What'd she say?"

Cindy answered, "Dunno. She said it way too fast."

"Us? What about him?" Jack demanded, pointing at his first victim, who responded with a "who me?" shrug.

"Me? What'd I do?" I said. I don't get in trouble. I've never even spoken to the vice-principal.

"YOU AND YOU, VICE-PRINCIPAL!" she said, pointing at Hud and me. "YOU GO TO THE NURSE!" she said, pointing at the kid who started it all.

Jack frowned. "Hud needs to go the nurse."

Cindy piped up. "No, I think I got that one. He's supposed to go to the nurse, and you two are in trouble."

Juan stepped in. "I got it that time. You guys go to the vice-principal, but Jack's right, you should stop by the nurse for an ice-pack." He looked at the other kid. "You need ice for your whole body."

Cindy, "What was that spark?"

"Come on, Jack, help me up. Let's go." My head was numb, and I let Jack pull me up.

"Sorry, Hud. Really."

"I know, Jack."

As we shuffled to the door, I hear Juan say, "I couldn't get a hand on him. What's with that?" followed by a girl's voice. "Miss Bangler, how are you going to get down from there?"

Feeling was returning to my face as we waited for the nurse; a steady throbbing settled in. Jack had lapsed into silence after a dozen apologies.

"Why do you do this, Jack? Getting hit hurts!"

Jack shrugged. "Other things hurt worse."

"That was bad. We're going to get a lot of questions about the force fields.

"Nah, by tomorrow they'll either forget or come up with their own answers. Force fields won't be one of them. Juan'll think he was too slow or something."

"What about the spark?"

"The lights flickered, who knows? Doesn't matter, we'll probably get suspended."

"Suspended? I've never been suspended before, Jack!"

"It can be a good thing, Hud. We can take Alice somewhere."

"My parents will hit the roof! I'll be grounded!"

"You already are, and you were keeping me out of trouble. Your folks'll understand."

He was probably right. "What about your dad?"

Jack sighed. "They'll give me a note, call Dad on a number that was disconnected a long time ago and the superintendent will tell Veep Brown to drive out and talk to my dad in person. Brown will say he did, but he won't. I'll be fine."

"Why won't he?"

"Because he did once."

Now we were waiting for VP Brown, me with an ice-pack on my face. My mother had been called and was on her way. I figured when she showed up, we'd go in, but I was wrong. Vice-Principal Brown opened his door and ushered us in.

I was shaking, too scared to speak.

VP Brown was a tall, stooped man with bushy hair and a mustache that drooped on either side of his mouth. He looked mournful but intimidating all at once, like a hound-dog with some bite left in him.

"Let's take a look, Hudson," he said.

I was surprised he knew my name. I dropped the ice-pack.

Brown whistled. Jack hunched lower in his seat. Brown cocked his head at Jack, thoughtfully.

"You two have been friends for a long time."

I nodded. Jack sunk lower.

"Who was the third party?" Brown said.

Neither of us said anything.

Brown leaned back in his seat, clasping his hands behind his head. "Let me guess. Someone insulted either your dad, Jack, or Hudson's mother."

My good eye got big.

"Hmmm, not Hudson's mother because you wouldn't jump in to break up that fight, so it was a careless remark about Jack's father, yes?"

I nodded mutely.

Brown leaned forward.

"Jack, you've never hit your friend before."

I looked at Jack. He was crying.

The phone buzzed on Brown's desk. He lifted the handset and listened. "Tell her I'll be right with her. Give me a few minutes. Thank you." He hung up.

"Your mother is here, Hudson, but I'd like you to stay here while Jack and I talk, OK?"

I nodded.

Brown came around his desk and leaned on it, reaching out for Jack's shoulder. I was alarmed for a moment, afraid the force field would block his touch. It didn't. Brown's hand settled on Jack's shoulder.

"This is different than all the other times you've been in here, isn't it, Jack?" He pulled a handkerchief from his jacket and offered it to Jack, who took it and scrubbed at his nose.

"I have to ask myself if this is an escalation," he continued. "We've talked about this, Jack. It's my job to prevent you from being a danger to the students and teachers here. Hudson, to catch you up on our conversations, I don't believe there's ever a reason for violence between children. There are enough adults around that if each of you would just come to one of us when you're being bullied, threatened, scared or otherwise in need, that fight would just go away.

"You need to understand that one of the great myths in humanity is the concept of us-and-them. Kids think adults are "them" not "us" and that bullies are "them." The truth is, every kid you call a bully is really someone else's victim. Of course, if you're being bullied, the thought that the bully is being abused by someone else holds little comfort, but because kids don't come to adults when they're bullied, neither bullied nor bully get the help they need. Adults are viewed as enemies or powerless. Neither is true.

"I've met Jack's dad." He shifted his attention from my wide-eyed expression to Jack.

"Jack, I think you're a remarkable young man." Jack's head came up in surprise. "Most of the kids who sit in that chair with a background like yours are the worst of bullies."

"Who has a 'background like me,' Mr. Brown?" Jack asked hollowly.

"Precisely like yours? None. I can think of several with worse."

Jack snorted. "Like who?"

Brown looked at the ceiling and exhaled slowly. "It's not my place to share that information with you."

Jack snorted again.

"But," Mr. Brown continued, "If it doesn't leave this room... Jack, I know I can trust you. Hudson?"

I nodded.

He nodded back. "Jason Pruitt."

I snorted.

Brown raised his eyebrow at me, and I wilted. "Jason is the youngest of eight boys. His father is a dim-witted man of the worse kind, who was beaten by his father. I know because the senior Pruitt and I went to school together. He beat me up regularly. Now he beats his kids regularly. The first time I called about Jason's violent tendencies, he said, 'which one is Jason?' I replied, 'the one all your other kids beat up on,' to which his reply was, 'Oh, that one.' He then called Jason an awful name, the same one he called me in school, and I'll tell you, it still burns now to hear it."

I'd never heard an adult talk like this before, like we were equals or something.

"Kids like Jack bully the bullies, standing up for themselves or often for other kids who can't or won't."

"That's Jack," I agreed, surprising myself that I could speak.

"He's still a bully, though," Mr. Brown said.

Jack sat up sharply.

"Do you deny it, Jack? Violence is your answer; violence is the voice of a bully, at this level or on the world stage. We have enough bullies, Jack. Strive for something different."

He picked up the phone. "Please send Mrs. Cook in."

He strode to the door as it opened and Mom stepped through, puzzlement clear on her face. Mr. Brown reached out and shook her hand. Her hand was in his when she saw me, the ice-pack and my swollen eye.

She rushed to me, holding me by the shoulders for closer inspection. Behind her, Jack was sitting rigidly with an emotion I'd never seen on his face: Terror.

"What happened!" she said, pulling me into a hug, which made my eye hurt worse.

Mr. Brown answered. "Seems Jack accidentally hit Hudson while aiming for someone else."

Mom swiveled to look at Jack. "You did this, Jack?"

Jack looked straight ahead, biting his lip, and nodded tersely.

"You poor baby!" and she enveloped him in a tight embrace.

Jack burst into tears of relief and I swear Mr. Brown was wiping moisture from his eyes.

Poor baby him? What about poor baby me? I'm the one with a black eye!

While Mom coaxed the story from Jack, Mr. Brown caught my attention.

"Consider what I said. Adults are not the enemy. No one is truly an enemy."

"Are we suspended?" I squeaked.

"For being friends? Never."

Later, after everything had been smoothed over and Mom asked Mr. Brown to call her for anything concerning me or Jack in the future, she drove us to my house, where we hung out in my room and I pressed more ice to my eye.

"You went to the moon again without me? You said you wouldn't do that anymore!"

"Technically, I said I wouldn't go to outer space without you. The Moon is near space," Jack said. Impressed he knew that despite myself, I shook it off.

"Jack....!"

He held up his hands in surrender.

"I couldn't get all that gold out of my mind, Hud, so I zipped up there, stripped it off the lander and brought it home."

"What about radiation?" I demanded.

"Alice checked it out. It was clean."

"How'd you get it off?"

"Tore it. It was pretty thin, really. It folded into a brick pretty easily."

"Then what?"

"Back to Earth and this morning I hit a pawn shop in Florida that buys gold."

"Florida? How'd you…"

"Dad's all about pawn shops; there's some good ones, but the kind I needed were in the skuzzy part of town, easy to find from the air."

"You took Alice out during the day?"

"Morning, always into the sun. She's good at stealth mode. Nobody sober saw us."

"And they just bought it, easy as pie?"

Jack stretched out on the bed while I grilled him from my desk chair.

"Well, it wasn't easy. They wanted to know where I got it, so I told them. Once they knew I was a smart-alec, it got easier. I pointed out it was thin, untraceable and easy to melt down and if they didn't like dealing with a kid, I'd go down the street and find someone who did."

I considered. "How much did you get?"

"Not as much as I should have, but we settled on five-hundred bucks."

"Five-hundred!"

"Four, now. I got stuff at K-Mart and stashed it in the barn."

"That's why you were late to school."

He grinned. "That and I had one of everything at McDonald's."

"OK, then," I said. "Next time, tell me first."

"Deal."

"So, tomorrow dinner with the 'rents, and Saturday..."

"Dinosaur Planet!" we chorused.

Best friends again; life was good.

Then Mom called up the stairs. "Hudson! A girl named Evangalina is here to see you!"

Jack elected to stay in my room after hooting and mock-choking himself. He could be such a kid sometimes.

Mom stood at the bottom of the stairs with her eyebrows raised in silent question. I shrugged in response.

Evangalina sat primly on the couch in our living room, flipping through a magazine and somehow taking up less space than she did in school.

"Hey," I said.

Her face brightened, then quickly clouded, when she saw my black eye. She rushed to me and clucked as she examined it from every angle.

"The weed did this?"

From up the stairs. "I ain't no weed!"

Her lids dropped. "It's here?"

"Jack's a he, not an it," I said, then shouted up the stairs, "go back to my room and shut the door, Jack!"

A slam echoed down the stairs in answer.

"It was an accident," I said to Evangalina.

"I heard all about it and just had to come over an' see for myself."

Mom was suddenly hovering at the kitchen entry. "Evangalina, would you like to help me prepare some finger sandwiches?"

Huh? "Finger sandwiches?" I mouthed without sound.

Evangalina clasped her hands at her chin. "I'd love to, Mrs. Cook! You have just the sweetest mom, Hudson!"

I glared at Mom as Evangalina skipped into the kitchen. She made a face in return.

"Ooooo!" trilled Evangalina from the kitchen. "A baby! I didn't know you had a baby sister, Hudson!"

I rolled my eyes and slumped into the kitchen where she was kitchy-cooing Ela.

"We eat finger sandwiches now?" I whispered to Mom.

She smiled and swatted at me as I passed.

"Would you like to mix the tuna salad or trim the crusts from the bread?"

The girlie stuff was too much for me, so I just parked on a stool and watched the mixing and slicing and dicing. The Evangalina I knew from school, all brash, demanding and sarcastic, had been replaced by a sweet, chatty girl I didn't recognize but kind of liked. Mom peppered her with questions about her family and interests and the usual parent standby, "what do you want to do when you grow up?" I learned more about her in a few minutes than I had all year at school.

When the tiny sandwiches were finally finished, Mom suggested calling Jack down. I opted to take a few "fingers" and a Coke to him.

"What's she want?" Jack said when I dropped off the snacks. "And what's with the tiny sandwiches?"

"I don't know."

"Which part?"

"Both parts," I said.

"Huh. Must be a girl thing," Jack said, stuffing two "fingers" in his mouth.

"Which part?" I said.

"Both parts," he said around tuna salad.

Downstairs, Evangalina was preparing to leave, hugging Ela and primly shaking Mom's hand.

"Walk me to the gate, Hudson?"

"We don't have a gate," I said.

"Hudson," Mom warned.

"I'll walk you to the sidewalk, I guess."

Mom piped up, "Do you need a ride home, dear?"

Evangalina smiled, "No thank you, Mrs. Cook, I live just a couple blocks over."

"You do?" I said.

"Hudson could walk you home," Mom volunteered.

"Just to the sidewalk is fine, thank you."

"All the same..." Mom started.

"The sidewalk is this way!" I said, opening the door and ushering her out.

"Go half way, Hudson, at least!" Mom called after us.

I sighed and kept going beyond the sidewalk. Evangalina walked quietly beside me.

I looked at her out of the side of my eyes. "Who are you and what have you done with Evangalina?"

She tittered. "Are you the same at school and at home with friends?"

"Pretty much."

"Well, you're not a girl."

I had no response to that. We walked in silence for a while.

"Sorry I wasn't there," Evangalina said.

"Why should you be?" I said.

"You kissed me, remember?" she said.

And there it was.

"Yeah, that. It was kind of like getting hit by Jack."

"What's that supposed to mean?"

"It was an accident."

Evangelina slowed down. "So, you don't like me." There was pain in her voice.

I thought about it.

"I like you a lot more now than I did then." I stopped and looked at her. "Which one of you am I supposed to like? The you at school or the you I'm with right now?"

We stood on the sidewalk looking at each other.

"That's a fair question," she allowed.

We resumed walking.

"This growing-up thing is harder than it looks," I said.

"I'll say," she said. "Hudson? Can we be friends this summer?"

"We are friends," I said.

"I mean the kind who do things in the summer."

"What kind of things?" I said, suspicious again.

"Things, you know. Swimming at the pool, movies, hanging at the mall."

"Just us?"

She rolled her eyes. "You can bring the weed and I'll bring friends."

"His name is Jack," I said. "Stop calling him 'weed!'"

"I can do that."

"It's demeaning," I said.

"Huh. You're right. I should know something about that." She said with surprise.

"Why?" I said.

"Because I'm black, Hudson." It was almost a whisper.

"So?"

"You mean that?"

And just like that, we were in the land of confusion again. "Mean what?"

"You don't care that I'm black?"

"Why should I?" I said.

"It matters to some people. Like Jack being poor."

"Jack's not poor," I scoffed. "I mean, he is, his dad is but..." I thought about picking up Big Jack from the bar and the way the bartender looked at us... no, not us, at Jack and his dad. About the way bigger kids teased Jack.

"Oh," I said. I was getting angry. "Is that why you're different at school?"

She smiled brilliantly and took my hand, melting away my anger. "See, you white kids ain't so dumb."

"So why do you like me if I'm white and you're black?"

She rolled her eyes theatrically. "If I have to tell you that, then you really are dumb!"

She yanked my arm, pulling me toward her, and kissed my cheek before running off.

Yep, I'm really dumb. And clueless.

As I walked home, I thought that might not be so bad sometimes, and absently rubbed my cheek.

CHAPTER 8

Revelations

S PORTING A BLACK EYE at school made me a hero
to everyone until last period in Miss Bangler's
Spanish class. The moo-moo was gone, replaced with a
dark pantsuit. She was in depressive mode again, placed
there by yesterday's fight. That meant workbooks out,
diagrammed sentences in Spanish on the board, and
very little talking from anyone. Miss Bangler prowled
through the rows, marking great slashes on people's
workbooks and grading accordingly in her black book.

What had promised to be the easiest class until
summer just became the hardest. Classmates glowered
at me and Jack, forgetting entirely the kid who lit the
fight's fuse.

Jack ignored them, and I slumped in my seat. Even Juan
glared at us, tinged with an edge of suspicion. At one

point, he leaned over to me and whispered, "How do you say 'untouchable' in Spanish?"

"I don't," I whispered back.

"He won't come, you know," Jack said as we walked home.

"He said that?" I asked.

"He showered this morning."

"My dad showers every morning."

"Mine doesn't."

"So maybe he'll come," I said.

"Not unless he's all liquored up."

"You don't know that," I said.

"Yeah, I do," he said, throwing a rock at a mailbox.

A few hours later, Big Jack proved him wrong. He showed up with a six-pack of beer with one missing, a jacket he looked uncomfortable in, and a badly shaved face.

Mom met him at the door with a big smile, as if he came over every week. She took his coat, deftly accepted the beer and pointed him out back to the barbeque and my dad.

Jack and I stayed in the kitchen and watched out the window. The men shook hands and Mom slipped out and handed Big Jack a lemonade with a paper umbrella in it. He looked at it in surprise, took an experimental sip and then drained the glass. He asked Mom a question, and she smiled and shook her head.

"He just asked for a beer," Jack said. "Your mom said 'no.' She's going to try to keep him sober all night. Good luck with that."

Dad held up a finger and handed Big Jack the spatula and dashed in past us for seasoning. Back out, he sprinkled it over the hamburgers but didn't take back the spatula. Big Jack, looking uncomfortable, started flipping the burgers after a prompt from Dad. The more he did, the more comfortable he got.

Mom appeared holding Ela, showing her off to Big Jack. The big man looked amazed.

"He didn't know about your sister," Jack said.

Mom held Ela out to Big Jack. Behind him, Dad looked alarmed. So did Big Jack. Mom smiled and put the baby in Big Jack's big hands.

"Jeez! Is she crazy?" Jack asked.

Ela looked small in his arms. He looked at her with a mix of pain and wonderment, cradling her carefully.

Jack sat up beside me. "Is he going to cry?"

He was blinking... Then he smiled crookedly at Mom and gave Ela back.

"A beer would go good with these," Big Jack said about the hamburgers.

We were seated around our picnic table under a high umbrella.

"I've got something better," Mom said, excusing herself. Big Jack looked relieved until she came back with a Dr. Pepper.

"The taste of summer," she said.

"Uh-huh," he said, cracking the can.

"I hope you're proud of your little man, here, Jack. He's a wonderful boy."

Big Jack regarded Little Jack and looked away. "I am. He's a good kid. Deserves better than me." He took a bite and looked at me. "How'd you get the shiner, Hud?"

I froze. Jack froze.

Mom to the rescue. "Boys will be boys."

Big Jack grunted. "You should look out for Hud, Jackie. See that doesn't happen."

"Sure thing, Dad."

"Been meaning to thank you for them new clothes you got Jackie. Shoulda gotten 'em myself. You all look out for him. I'm grateful," he said, looking at his plate.

Mom and Dad exchanged surprised glances. Of course, that's how Jack explained his new clothes.

"Glad to help, Jack," Dad said. "That's what friends are for."

Big Jack squinted at them. "No, it's more than that. Every day I expect Social Services to come collect the boy.

Every day I'm surprised they don't. You know, a beer would sure be good right now."

Jack sat woodenly, not eating his food. I'd stopped as well.

"He's your son, Jack," Dad said.

"You've thought about it, though," Big Jack said. "Either calling them or just keeping him yourselves. I know you have. You probably should." Now Big Jack wasn't eating. He was hunched over his plate, looking for words in the pattern.

"You've lost enough, Jack," Mom said. "And you're doing your best."

He looked up at her with hooded eyes. "My best? It's all I can do not to go in there and drain each beer can until I can't see anymore. I haven't done my best since Jackie's mother died. 'Bout all I can say is that I've never hit him, right Jackie?"

Jack just sat there.

"Jackie?"

Even Ela was quiet.

Big Jack looked from Mom to Dad, then back at Jack. "I've never hit you, Jackie."

Jack swallowed hard. "Never on purpose, Dad."

"Never..." Big Jack was breathing hard, looking at each of us, then somehow he pulled back into himself, shaking his head. He pushed out from the table, knocking his chair over and bolting from the table, through the house toward the door.

Dad followed quickly, catching him before he reached the door and pulled him to the living room out of our sight.

"Jack," Mom said. "Why haven't you ever told us?"

"Why haven't you told ME?" I demanded.

"I want to go home now."

Mom circled the table and cradled Jack's head. "After all these years, you still don't know this is your home, too?"

For the first time ever, Jack didn't melt under Mom's embrace. He remained wooden, unapproachable.

Chapter 9

Tyrannosaurus Rat

"**C**OME OOOOON, JACK, WE'RE going to the Dinosaur Planet!" I prodded.

We were really cruising. I think. There wasn't much out here, just the unmoving stars, but when we zoomed past Pluto... at least I think it was Pluto. It could have been a big asteroid... it was there and gone in a blink. Leaving Earth and blipping past the moon was as nauseating as normal, but out here, it was kind of peaceful and quiet. Too quiet. Jack had barely spoken.

"Maybe we'll see one kill something," Jack said flatly.

Ooookay.

"This is a good thing, Jack."

He shrugged. "I like dinosaurs."

"Not dinosaurs, you goof, your dad."

Big Jack was in rehab, Jack was living with us for a week or so, to "get past the worst part," whatever that means.

Jack leveled a sullen look at me. "It won't work."

"My dad said it would, but it might be rocky for a while."

Jack turned away. "Believe it when I see it."

Before I could respond, Alice's control panel lit up, blue lights flashing beneath the surface.

"That's new," Jack said.

And then we folded, and the universe disappeared!

I couldn't see, feel, smell, hear, or anything. It felt like not existing... except I liked it! Something else kicked in, an awareness of fullness... of excitement. There was nothing, but there was everything!

And then we were back, just somewhere else. A weird, dusty-looking solar system spread beneath us with a sun that had a bulging ring around it. A dozen gas giants glowed brightly within the glowing backdrop of the system.

I spun to scream at Jack, but he wasn't there. What? My eyes swept down and found Jack in a ball, retching.

"Jack?" He flinched when I put my hand on his shoulder.

Huffing, he uncurled, and his eyes were saucers. Clutching his stomach, he spoke in a trembling voice, cautious about throwing up. "That. Was. Awful."

"The thing? That was great!"

"You nuts? I don't even know how to describe it!"

He climbed to shaky feet.

"Try," I said.

He shook his head. "I don't know, it was like freezing and burning all at once, only... is that what it's like to be alone?"

"Alone? Hey, Alice, stop for a minute."

"Yeah. Like, empty... or... I'm not doing that again."

"We have to get home, Jack."

"What was it like for you?"

I tried to get that feeling back. "It was like being connected to everything. It was... wonderful."

"Freak," Jack said. "Whoa!" He'd finally looked around.

While our solar system was stark and barren, this one seemed filled with fairy dust. We were parked "above" the disk-shaped ring of worlds, the sun's gravity and spin holding it flat and contained within the emptiness of space. Its beauty touched the fading sense the "other space" had inspired, leaving me a little bit sad, but it revived Jack.

"Dinosaurs, Alice?"

Alice holo-ed a double-thumbs up and we were in motion again, dropping down, watching the glowing disk grow and envelop us. Once inside, the "glowing dust" wasn't as apparent. We didn't see it as much as recognize the difference from our system. There were no shadows anywhere on Alice, while back home, great long shadows always stretched away from our sun.

A gas giant sped by, and then another. Then we were beyond the outer worlds and cruising for a while before a planet suddenly appeared with no warning. We'd grown used to seeing planets outlined against the sun or blocking stars, but here in the murk, planets just popped out of the bright "gloom."

As we drew near, we saw the planet was all a shimmering green-and-brown.

"No oceans," Jack said.

I squinted. "Maybe the water's green here. It's moving."

"Don't think so. Looks like all land. The shimmer must come from the air. Find a dinosaur, Alice!"

We zoomed into the atmosphere, only it wasn't atmosphere. It was vapor so thick it beaded up on Alice's force field. And then we were through and the shimmer disappeared.

"It's a vapor canopy!" I said.

"A what?" Jack squinted at me.

We'd learned about vapor canopies in Sunday School, when our youth pastor got on his Creation kick, telling us it was "only a theory." It wasn't worth trying to explain to Jack, though. He'd just call me a freak again.

Land became giant trees that spread wide. As we dropped into them, it was stunning. These trees made our redwoods look puny. Their branches seemed to reach for miles.

"Dinosaur, Alice," Jack said with impatience.

"But not too close," I said.

"Wimp," Jack said.

We saw a strange-looking tree shaking from above and Alice circled it, dropping beneath the canopy amidst giant, leathery, hanging fruit. She hovered.

Jack laughed. "What the heck is that!"

He pointed. I joined him in laughing. It looked like a huge, dumpy rat with an enormous head. It reminded me of Templeton in the Charlotte's Web video after he'd gorged at the fair. A vast rat tail spiraled on the ground, balancing the creature's bulk. It was hard to judge scale, but Alice seemed about the size of its porridge head as it rooted around, trying to snag an orb. Finally, it succeeded, pulling it down and swinging the stem into its tiny hands. From there, the rat-thing began chomping with surprisingly fearsome teeth. Biting through the leathery skin, it pulled people-sized seeds out and swallowed them whole, where they must have spiraled down into its vast rounded bulk. Its belly was so big it reached all the way down to clawed feet that gripped the ground as it pulled the fruit down. Its dimpled flesh had no hair, giving it a moist, bread-like look.

"I wanted to see a dinosaur, Alice, not a naked rat!" Jack said.

Alice flashed a double-thumbs up.

"That's no dinosaur! I wanted to see a giant lizard!"

Alice holo-ed the rat-thing, then erased the heaving flesh and rendered its skeleton in blue light.

My skin pebbled.

"That's a T-Rex," I said.

"No way!" Jack shouted.

It wasn't a perfect match, but it was very close.

"Alice, did our dinosaurs look like that?"

A perfect T-Rex appeared before the super-rat skeleton. There were differences; shape of the head, angle of the hip, but they could have been related. A DNA spiral appeared before both of them and each "fleshed up," layering muscle and fat and flesh. Once skin wrapped around them both, they were almost identical.

"That's not a T-Rex, Alice! We have pictures," Jack said.

"No, we have drawings, Jack, something an artist made up from the bones," I said, trying to keep the wonder out of my voice.

"That isn't a dinosaur!"

"What's the difference? You wanted to see something huge; now you have."

Jack spun toward me, real anger shaking his voice. "I didn't want to see something big. I wanted to see something dangerous! Not this, this, thing. Does it even eat meat, Alice?"

Two-thumbs down glowed in the air.

"Well, T-Rex ate other dinosaurs; he chased 'em and ate 'em!"

"We don't know that, Jack. No one's ever seen one. Until now."

"No way! Don't we have some from, like, mud pits or something?"

"Tar pits, and I think the only whole ones were Woolly Mammoths and they look like shaggy elephants."

Jack's eyes narrowed. "Those weren't dinos, though."

"No, but if we only had bones, who knows what we'd think they look like?"

"What about Godzilla?"

"Make-believe, Jack."

Dejected, we looked over the jungle again. "What's that?" Jack said, pointing.

An outcropping I'd mistook for rocks was slithering backward, drawing an immense neck from a crevasse in the green jungle floor. The rat-thing took notice and waddled over, shifting from clawed foot to clawed foot. Finally, a dripping head withdrew atop a vast neck. The pudgy body shook, and the neck rose from its shoulders, drawing a huge arc before the head began to rise. The rat-thing waddled under the rising head and tilted its great jaws upward, the water streaming from the serpent-cow's mouth dropping straight into the rat-thing's throat. It was like a momma bird feeding its baby bird.

The rat-thing had to shuffle forward to stay under the stream, its stubby arms waving as if in a bad balancing act.

Finally, the great head reached the top of the arch and tilted upward. Rat-thing hopped around, hoping for more. Instead, we heard gurgling as the remaining water in the serpent-cow's mouth and neck sloshed down into its body, its white, naked flesh quivering as gallons of water passed.

Jack slumped down onto Alice's floor. "Take me home, Alice."

"What's your beef, Jack?" I asked. I thought it was cool.

Jack looked at me balefully. "It's like finding out Superman's a wimp. No! It's like finding out Batman's really a fat, little bald guy with a good publicist."

"What's the big deal? So, the books are wrong. We know the truth now! That's pretty cool!"

"You make me go to school, right? But everything we're learning there is wrong! I'm wasting my time. YOU'RE wasting my time. Home, Alice."

"Look, Jack, our dinos could be reptilian. They probably had to face the sun. These guys don't. The canopy filters out the damaging sun beams."

Jack's chin dipped low, like when he planned on attacking someone.

"Fine!" I said, throwing my hands in the air. "Take us home, please, Alice."

Jack was too depressed to even notice us rising from the jungle, the disappointing dinosaurs watching us go. I noticed, though, my knuckles going white on the railing. They stayed that way until the planet fell behind us, making me less dizzy. Jack stayed seated on the floor.

"School isn't just for learning facts, Jack. My Dad says school is more about learning to ask questions than just scoring the answers. He says the newest discoveries are because scientists are finally figuring out what questions to ask."

"Maybe that's what school is to you. It just makes me feel dumber than I already am."

I shrugged. "Forget about all that, then. School is where we hang out with friends."

Jack looked up at me, then away. "You're my only friend, Hud."

"That's not true!" But I knew it was.

He offered a weak smile. "I have Alice now, right, Alice?"

When two-thumbs up glowed in the air, we both laughed.

Then Jack tilted his head. "Are you alive, Alice?"

I jerked back. Alice was a machine, not a person.

One thumbs-up and one thumbs-down glowed.

"Sort of?" I asked.

Two thumbs-up.

"What does sort-of mean?"

Jack popped out another surprising question: "Alice, were you lonely before we found you?"

Two thumbs-up. Yes.

Jack stroked the railing. "I'm sorry." Then to me: "Maybe there is something about this question thing."

Lights began to blink rapidly beneath the control-panel surface. Jack jumped up.

"Wait! Stop, Alice!"

The blinking stopped.

"What?"

"I don't wanna go through that... that... whatever place!"

"We have to, Jack. That's how we get home."

Jack looked away.

"What if we hold hands?" I blurted.

Jack scowled at me.

I put my hands up. "OK, OK, sorry I asked."

"That'd be weird, is all."

I nodded. He was right. I threw an arm around Jack's shoulder, "Punch it, Alice!"

Jack stiffened, lights blinked, and we were gone.

I couldn't feel Jack, not in the usual way, as the everything engulfed us. Before it was like touching all, and it still was, but it was also like feeling a small bubble of nothing near me. That must have been Jack. I was happy and worried at the same time; happy because this felt wonderful, worried about Jack, but all of it in a way that wasn't thinking or feeling. There was no passage of time; it could be a blink or a lifetime...

...and then we were out!

Only this wasn't right, this wasn't home. Billows of sparkling clouds spiraled away and red/purple lights raced across Alice's board! Lightning split the clouds and for the first time on Alice, I could feel pulling! Jack grabbed my shoulder and pointed! The spiraling columns stretched and disappeared into a great black nothing... a meteor bounced off Alice as she strained to pull away from the pull, force field sparking with blue flashes...

"That's a black hole!" I shouted. Light was violently being wrenched around us and the cloud stuff streamed by, but it was eerily silent, no thunder, no rushing wind, just an overwhelming sensation of force.

Jack screamed, "Alice! What are you doing!"

Was she broken? Were we trapped out here? My parents will never know where we are!

Alice responded with a blue circle in front of us, then zoomed what she was looking at so we could see it.

A ship!

There was an alien ship out there!

"Alice?" Was she taking us to her people? Were we going to be slaves? Or eaten?

The image of the ship hung in the zooming circle. We looked closer. A single blip pulsed inside.

"Is someone trapped on that ship?" Jack said.

Two thumbs-up.

"You want to rescue him?"

Two more thumbs-up.

"Jack?" He was grinning!

"This is more like it!" he said, slapping his thigh! "Isn't this great?"

"No! Look behind us, Jack, that's a black hole trying to suck us in and crush us! This is anything but all right!"

"Man up, Hud! This is an adventure!"

I could see the real ship, now, a steadily growing speck. Looking back at the zoomed image, it was an odd shape, with a rounded front and honeycombed sides. I hoped they weren't insect people. The rear was damaged; the structures scored and burned.

Jack pointed at one of the honeycombs. All the others were empty, but one was still filled with something.

"Think that means anything?" he said.

I wasn't thinking at all! My head swiveled from the holo-ship, to the real ship, to the black hole and the swirling mass it was consuming.

The real ship was growing bigger, tumbling through space. It was traveling with the streaming columns of star-stuff further out, which means it was rushing toward us as we rushed to it. It was aiming for the black hole and so would we, unless Alice could pull it out. When I asked, she gave me two shaking thumbs-up.

A panel opened, and another bracelet emerged.

I shook my head. "I'm not going in there." The zoomed image disappeared as the real ship became the same size. It zoomed past and Alice raced back to catch up, the black hole looming way ahead, but I didn't know how far ahead...

The honeycombs blurred by until we matched speeds, then Alice ducked into one. She docked by thrusting us into the hole at the back, almost a perfect fit for Alice's base. We were now inside the ship!

"No choice, bud. You're already here. Of course, you could stay here, like a wimp, but I'm going. Point the way, Alice!"

Great, Jack was going all Indiana Jones! He stuffed the new bracelet in his pocket and held up his. The glowing wart popped up, and he suddenly had a glowing arrow pointing the way. He ran through an opening that opened like a yawning mouth, not a door.

I closed my eyes. Then I ran after him, hoping no teeth waited beyond.

Chapter 10

To the Rescue

J ACK RACED AHEAD, DOWN a large tube-like corridor. It was dark, but square panels that looked like portholes dotted the wall. They glowed faintly but cast no light.

"Jack! Can you hear that?" I yelled.

He stopped and turned back to me, squinting. "Sorta. That squealing? I hear it more with my teeth than with my ears."

"Slow down, huh?" I was feeling edgy, like my nerves were dancing. I mean beyond the usual terrified jumpiness. The place just felt... wrong...

I caught up with Jack. He grabbed my shirt at the shoulder and tugged me after him.

"I think we have to go up, look for stairs or an elevator or something."

That's when we fell down a shaft. In the gloom, we just ran out over nothing and just as we realized we were falling, with that gut dropping lurch, we were rising again, falling upward!

"Stop screaming!" Jack shouted.

I shut my mouth. Hadn't realized I was, but my throat was raw so I took his word for it.

We fell up faster, then slowed, hanging in nothing, then up we went again.

"What..."

"Shhhh!" Jack said. "I'm counting."

My arms were pinwheeling to keep me upright, and he was counting!

"This one!" He grabbed me and leaned forward and something-that-was-nothing nudged us into a new corridor.

"How'd you know..."

He cut me off with a slashing motion at his neck. Then he pointed down the hallway to a doorway that was casting blue light.

The alien was in there!

That terrible keening sounded out again, making us grit our teeth.

"What is that?" Jack whispered.

"Ship status terminal." It felt like when Alice translated our Spanish teacher's language, in our bones.

I grabbed Jack. "The ship's in trouble!" I rasped.

"No duh, Hud, there's a black hole outside!" He rolled his eyes and crept slowly forward, grabbing me again to make me go with him. Something with wings was trying to burst from my throat, I didn't know if it was crazy laughter or uncontrollable sobbing, so clamped my jaw to keep it in.

Jack reached the edge of the door. Before looking around, he held his hand in front of his face. He was checking to see if his force field was on! Good idea! I shoved him to see if it was on and ended up pushing him in front of the door.

He froze. Looked back at me with imploring eyes.

I bit my lip. Seemed like a good idea at the time...

Jack swung his gaze into the room, squinted, then pulled up. We beckoned me to look.

I edged just my eyes past the doorframe, trying to see everything at once.

A curved window showed the terrors of space and swirling death beyond the glass. All around the near-empty room was what at first looked like candles but weren't. Instead of flame, an orb of blue light hovered over a jar or a candlestick attached to the struts of the window.

Between the middle-most "candles" a robed figure bent over the floor as if praying. Or maybe that was the alien's shape.

Before Jack could speak—he was opening his mouth—I squeaked. I'd been doing that a lot lately. I'd try to say an everyday word and my voice would turn into a squeak. I don't think I was trying to talk this time, though. It came unbidden. Jack glared at me.

"Ship status terminal!" The keening and translation came at the same time, this time.

The figure straightened up, then stood, still looking out the window. The wide shoulders dropped as if squaring up. I could tell the head under the hood tilted up. At full height, it was still a head shorter than us. I thought of Jawas from Star Wars and squeaked again.

Jack slugged me.

The figure pivoted.

Then it took a step back, clearly surprised.

Even with the light of the candles, the face under the hood was set in shadows.

That head tilted, and it stepped forward.

We stepped backward.

It stopped and stubby hands reached from under the sleeves to pull back the hood. I bit my lip, afraid of some hideous, bulbous face.

"It's Flipper," Jack said.

It kind of was.

Shiny, blue-white skin on a smooth dome, large black eyes and a slight, blunt dolphin-like beak with an upturned smile... it did look like Flipper, only wider.

We were completely disarmed. When it tilted its head to look us over, the smile didn't leave, but its torpedo chest began to rise and fall rapidly. It shied away from us, but it still took us a moment to realize it was scared of us. Its beak opened and our teeth buzzed as high keening pops and grunts jumped in and out of our hearing range, followed a half-step by Alice's translation. "You are not Aphani."

"Ship status terminal. Atmosphere purging!" grated the ship.

The alien's eyes grew wider still and four-fingered hands reached for its thick neck.

"The thing," I urged Jack, without taking my eyes away from the small alien.

"Right." He dug the wristband out of his pocket and held it out. The alien began to gasp but refused to move toward us. Jack knelt, put it on the ground and shoved it toward the small person. It stopped at the alien's feet.

A three-toed foot scooted out from under the hem, deftly snatched up the still-flat wristband and passed it to a stubby hand, which slapped it onto its other wrist.

The wristband obediently shaped itself around the thick blue-white arm. Clearly, the alien was familiar with the device.

We continued to stare at each other. It inhaled deeply.

The alien's mouth opened, our teeth buzzed, and Alice supplied a voice.

"You are not Aphani."

"What's an Aphani?" I shouted.

"This ship detected an Aphani Personal Transportation Platform."

"That's ours. Her name is Alice. I'm Jack. This is Hud."

"Why do you have an Aphani device if you are not Aphani?"

"We found it."

Its head tilted. "Found it?"

"In a cave. On Earth. We... don't know what Aphani are or what happened to them. We're humans," I said.

"I do not know of your people."

"We didn't know about yours, either," Jack said.

It looked out the window, at the black hole.

"There are none of my people left but me."

I jumped.

"We have to get out of here!"

"What do you intend to do with me?"

"Save you?"

"For what?"

It was awfully calm, considering the destruction outside.

"For what what?" I said. "To save you."

"For enslavement?"

"No."

"For consumption?"

"Huh?" Jack said.

"No!" I said. "It's afraid we want to eat it."

"No!" Jack said. "You don't want to eat us, do you?"

A deep thrumming came from the alien.

"We have to go!" I urged.

The alien bobbed. "I thought my story was over. I guess not." It pulled off the robe, revealing a baggy jumpsuit over a torpedo body. The legs were very short, but its waist was higher on its body, as if most of the legs were inside its torso.

It padded toward us and we all turned to run down the corridor. It ran slower than we did.

"Ship status terminal. Atmosphere zero. Simulated gravity diminishing. Inertial generators approaching inoperability."

"Wha....!" Our steps turned into a great leap and my stomach lurched as we rebounded off the ceiling and walls.

The alien sailed past us with a strange grace, pirouetting and beckoning to us.

"We must hurry! If the I-Gens shut off... we must be on your Alice before that happens!"

We grabbed at the odd lights to stop our tumble.

"What are I-Gens?" shouted Jack as we scrabbled over the wall.

"Rotating Gravity Generators that prevent everything from crashing against the wall whenever we change course, accelerate or decelerate. If they shut off, we'll be squashed into pulp!"

We crawled faster, grabbing for handholds. The alien seemed to dance, barely touching the walls to keep going.

We sailed past the elevator shaft, but the alien plucked at our sleeves and dragged us down. I felt spinny for a moment because "up" and "even" were the same.

Jack flew by me. "It's like swimming!"

That helped. I began to push off like I was in a pool.

"What is swimming?" asked the alien.

"You know, like this only in water," Jack said. We're moments from dying and they're having a conversation! Was I the only one who got the danger we were in?

The alien tinkled out laughter again. "As if there could ever be that much water."

Ship status terminal. Inertial Generators failing in 5, 4, 3..."

TO THE MOON, ALICE!

"Here! We're here!" Jack yelled, pushing the alien through the hatch to Alice and reaching back to me. I grabbed his hand, and he pulled...

"...1."

Gravity returned in a dozen different directions at once and I slammed against the hatch, my force field flaring bright as the sun, then I was on Alice crowding in with Jack and the alien as she spun away from the ship at dizzying speed, the great ship falling away. Alice shook violently, her force field becoming visible as it stretched toward the hungry black hole. The alien squealed, and we saw its ship crumple and collapse while simultaneously stretching toward the hole.

In movies, there would be scary music. Other than the alien keening, the vast destruction was utterly silent as vast chunks of rock—a former planet?—twisted into ugly shapes that looked wrong.

Alice was straining, her bubble flaring. We were in danger of becoming part of the cosmic destruction, but all we could see was the hungry maw of the black hole. None of us noticed Alice's panel dancing with blue light.

And then there was nothing.

The in-between space was shocking, sensory deprivation after sensory overload. I found myself uncomfortable with peace, the "all-ness" a struggle to feel...

...and then we were out, into normal space.

I sighed. Jack shuddered. The alien sighed and... purred.

"Man! I hate that!" Jack said, gritting his teeth.

The alien tilted its head. "You hate para-space? You reject peace and stillness?"

"Para-space?" I said. "That's what you call it?"

"Some call it jump-space or fold-space. It is the principle means of long distance space travel. Your Alice is very advanced. I've never seen a PTP this small and powerful. It pulled away from a black hole in one piece! The jump was momentary... far too short to feel the One's happiness."

"Nothing happy about it. It feels... hungry to me." Jack said.

The all-black eye rolled toward me.

"I like it," I said, shrugging my shoulders.

Jack punched my shoulder. "Not me, man, not me." His mood flipped like a pancake, turning hyper in a heartbeat. "The rest of it, though? That rocked! We're like space heroes, rescuing aliens," he stabbed a finger at our new passenger. "That's YOU... from certain doom!" he said, letting his voice echo on the last word.

The platform seemed too small for Jack, who danced wildly without getting too close to the alien. Jack crowed at me, then abruptly stopped, staring past me with wide eyes.

"Hud, where are we?" he said, "And what is that?"

I looked around. A giant white rock streamed bright vapor in front of it was off and below our left side and it was growing bigger.

"I think it's a comet." Far behind us was either a small sun or a large star. "It's leaving the orbit of that star, so the tail is in front of it."

"Why is it getting bigger?"

"We're landing on it," squeaked the alien.

"Alice, we want to go home," Jack prompted.

"No, wait, Jack. We have to figure out where... Um, what's your name?"

Alice had no translation for the Pop-Pop-Squeal the alien offered.

Jack tried to mimic it and failed. "How about Porpi? That's close," he said.

"Jaccccckkkkk!" I moaned.

He fish-eyed at me.

I fish-eyed back. "Porpi – porpoise – dolphin..." I jerked my head at the Flipper-like alien.

The alien, through Alice's translation, said, "Porpi is fine. I will be Porpi to you."

"Naw," Jack said, "It sounds like a girl's name."

"It is fitting, then. I am a girl."

Jack rolled his eyes. "Figures."

"OK, Porpi," I said, cutting off further Jack-isms. "Where do we take you?"

"I think your Alice is taking all of us there," she said, pointing to the comet.

"Alice!" Jack said, "Home!"

"I believe Alice is damaged. Is this correct, Alice?" Porpi purred.

A blue thumbs up ghosted and flickered over the panel.

Panic seized my heart. "What's wrong, Alice?"

Her hologram flickered and failed.

"Does Alice not speak?" Porpi asked.

"She was shot by Tonto," Jack said.

Porpi's head tilted.

"Like, a hundred years ago, Alice had an accident. The... Aphani? were hurt and Alice hid in a cave until we found her. I don't know what happened to the Aphani." I said. "Alice, will you be able to fix yourself?"

No hologram displayed.

The comet was getting close.

"What's wrong with her?" Jack said, worry tingeing his voice.

Porpi answered. "If Alice works like the Personal Transport Platforms I've seen, she runs on gravity skids. It is possible the gravity skids are out of sync. But, then again, she is far more advanced than any I have seen, so she may run on different principles. Self-repair may be possible." The alien appeared un-rattled about the danger.

"She couldn't fix her talker," Jack pointed out.

"Her communicator is a physical module; gravity skids are virtual devices," Porpi said.

"What's 'virtual' mean?" I said.

"They are made of an energy matrix. The massive gravity of the black hole disrupted the matrix. Alice must re-knit another."

The comet rushed up toward us, too fast. "Hold on!" Jack yelled.

Alice impacted hard, knocking us into one another. Porpi ended up on top of me while Jack tumbled off Alice altogether.

Porpi smiled down at me, massive eyes blinking, and pushed easily to drift away from me. There was almost no gravity.

"Jack! Hold on to something so you don't drift away!" I rolled to get eyes on Jack. He was on all fours, staring at the tail steam surrounding us. The horizon all around us was streaming vapor moving very fast.

"That looks dangerous," he said.

"It is," I said. "The star's heat is melting the comet's ice coating, and it streams away from the solar wind. We're in the lee of the comet, like the eye of a hurricane, so we should be fine."

"Unless the comet is rotating," Porpi volunteered. "Then we will eventually turn toward the heat of the star. These lifebands are much smaller than the ones I have seen. I wonder if it could withstand that much heat. Though certainly, it wouldn't matter, the jet stream will blow us from the comet."

"Let's hope it isn't rotating, then," Jack said.

Porpi was squinting toward the stars we could see. "If we were, would you want to know?"

Jack and I looked at each other.

"No," I said at the same time Jack said, "Yes."

He punched me.

"OK," I said, "Yes."

"We are rotating," Porpi said.

I squeaked.

"Very slowly."

"We're going to die," I said.

"Perhaps Alice will be repaired by then," she said.

"Can we do anything?" Jack said.

Porpi began singing in her pops and whistles, either too fast for the... lifebands... to translate, or perhaps they were untranslatable. I didn't know if she was happy or if her big black eyes and naturally-upturned mouth forced a smile around her snout. Her torso swayed to her song, and she stepped off the platform, her force field parting the mist as she wandered off.

Jack leaned toward me. "What's it doing?"

I leaned back. "I'm not sure, but I think she is praying."

Jack scoffed. "That's not praying. It sounds... chipper. Maybe she's crazy."

The singing stopped. "I can hear you," lilted her voice. She turned in the mist and her eyes glimmered with amusement. I think.

"Are you praying?" I said.

"Of course. All beings pray." I found myself smiling, returning hers. Then I felt stupid because for all I knew, that was her way of frowning.

"Jack doesn't," I said.

"Why would Jack not pray?"

"He doesn't believe in God."

Porpi blinked. "Of course Jack does."

I shook my head. "He doesn't."

"I'm right here. You can ask me."

Porpi looked at him. "Is this true?"

"Yes."

Porpi considered. "Are you defective?"

"No!"

Porpi shifted those black eyes to me. "How is this possible?"

"A lot of people don't believe in God!" Jack said.

I waved my hand at them. "Now is not the best time for this conversation. We're going to die!"

Porpi edged further away from us. "Do you believe in the One, Hudson?"

"The One? You mean God? Yes. Absolutely."

"I will pray. You will join me?"

"Yes, and so will Jack," I said.

"No, Jack won't," Jack said.

Porpi reared back from him. "Is he dangerous?" Porpi asked.

"Only if you push him too far," I said.

Porpi edged further away from him.

Jack huffed and climbed up on Alice. Porpi wandered over the blasted landscape. The ice beneath us wasn't slippery, or maybe the force fields kept us from sliding. It looked like a frozen desert with mounds of twisted ice, some small, others towering. The alien moved easily in low gravity.

I got on my knees by a couch-sized bump where the mist wasn't too thick and folded my hands. I prayed silently until a song of squeaks and sighs danced along my bones. Porpi stood with arms stretched out and beak to the sky.

TO THE MOON, ALICE!

This was what a whale would sound like singing in air instead of water. It was haunting and beautiful. My prayer seemed pale in comparison.

Jack came bounding over to us. "Hey! Alice's hologram is working again!"

Porpi turned serenely and waddled past Jack. "There you have it. Prayer is effective."

Jack rolled his eyes and scrambled past Porpi. He jumped up on Alice.

"Alice, you feeling better?" he asked.

One Thumbs Up and one Thumbs Down.

"Can you make yourself all better, Alice?" I asked.

Thumbs up.

"How long will it take?" I asked.

A hologram of the Earth appeared, and a circle scribed almost all the way around it. Say twenty hours.

"That's almost a whole day! Jack, my parents are going to kill me!"

Porpi cleared her throat. "Alice, how long before we rotate into the comet tail?"

Another circle scribed outside the repair circle and stopped just before the other ended. Nineteen and a half hours.

"So we're going to die," I said, sitting heavily on Alice's floor.

ROBERT ALEXANDER SWANSON

A holographic hand waggled a scary "maybe."

Chapter 11

Chillin' on a Comet

"**I**'M HUNGRY," JACK SAID. He'd wandered off to an ice mound fifty yards away, but I heard him through the lifeband as if he were beside me.

My stomach growled in agreement.

It didn't matter. We'd die of... of... comet tail before we could starve.

I was sitting on a ball of ice billions of miles from home, almost certainly going to die... and it didn't seem real. I couldn't even see our sun, let alone Earth from here. Not that I'd know where to look. I'd never see Mom, Dad or Ela again. I'd never go to school or graduate college. All I felt was numb.

At least we had a soundtrack. Porpi had been singing for the last hour, wandering across the face of the comet. Maybe that was why I wasn't crying in terror.

"Hey, Alien!" Jack shouted. "Do you have to do that?"

The keening song cut off. Porpi turned and tilted her head at Jack, her permanent smile didn't hide the apprehension in her eyes. "I do not."

"Good then," Jack huffed and turned away.

"You know, to Porpi, we're the aliens, Jack."

"I ain't no alien!"

I rolled my eyes. "It's just a matter of perspective, Jack."

He didn't turn around.

Porpi sidled closer to me. I smiled at her.

"I am sorry," Porpi said, moving off.

"No, wait! Yes, you can sit with me! That's why I smiled."

"Smile?"

"This." And I smiled at her. "This means, well, a lot of things, but happiness, approval, stuff like that."

"In my culture, baring your teeth is a form of anger or warning. Like this." Her lips peeled way back, revealing large, sharp teeth, transforming her dolphin face into a vicious snarl. I jerked back, and in the low gravity arced into the air, making me flail wildly.

Jack laughed.

Porpi turned in surprise. "Jack, you are praying!"

"That's laughing! Man! Can't a guy make a sound?" He stalked further away as I recovered.

"Don't do that again, okay? That was scary," I said.

Her snout dipped. I couldn't help it. Her unintentional smile and wide eyes gave her a mirthful look and I laughed.

"This is laughter?"

"Uh-huh. Do you laugh?"

"I do. It is not so musical, though. It sounds like an old-style engine."

"Can you laugh for me?" I said.

Porpi turned away.

It suddenly occurred to me her human-like smile didn't mean anything.

"Porpi. Are you sad?"

She didn't say anything, just looked up into the ring of sky we could see. I followed her gaze. What I had thought was an effect of the comet was, I realized, the smeared remains of the solar system we had just left. I couldn't see the black hole, of course, just the plasma smear streaming toward it.

"All my people have found the answer to the cosmic question. What is on the other side of a black hole?"

"Maybe they survived."

"They did not."

"I'm sorry, Porpi."

She turned to me. "When it is time, none may forestall it; when it is time; peace follows."

Jack's voice thrilled through the lifebands. "Hud! Porpi! We're in trouble!"

In the distance, he stood atop an ice hill, waving us to hurry.

On instinct, I took a single running step and flew into the air. Porpi neatly grabbed my foot and somehow glided to Jack, with me in tow. A well-calculated leap placed her, and me, beside Jack.

"You're such a doof, Hud. Look."

He pointed into a diamond valley, facets gleaming everywhere.

"Cool," I said.

"Not so cool, Hud. They're moving. This way."

I looked closer. The things I'd mistaken for large diamonds were moving in waves toward us. As they got closer, horror spread over me.

"Are those cockroaches?"

"There's millions of 'em. Big, glass cockroaches."

They were swarming up our ice hill. I turned to run, but Jack grabbed me.

"Force fields. Chill."

He was right. Our fields were apparently set at "balloon" because the ice bugs parted in a wide circle around us, drifting higher and higher until they were swarming over our protective force bubbles. We were buried in bugs!

TO THE MOON, ALICE!

"Shut up, Hud!"

I'd been screaming. Enough so my throat hurt. Why was I the only one freaked out? Okay, Jack is crazy, but why was Porpi so serene?

She looked at me with one great eye. "The One is good." Then her gaze went back to the bugs.

Walking toward Alice while we were buried in bugs was impossible. Porpi reached out, joining her field with ours and grabbed our arms. Then she leaped.... And we were moving! Once the field left the ground, bugs poured underneath and carried us in their clutches!

"What if they take us underground!" I screamed.

Porpi tilted her head at me. "They are taking us to Alice."

"How do you know that?" I shouted.

"Isn't it obvious? Alice called them."

Jack scoffed. "Alice called bugs?"

"These are not bugs, Jack, they are miners."

"Huh?"

"Robots."

"Why are robot cockroaches on a comet?" he said.

"They are comet miners. Seeded millennia ago by my ancestors. Comets such as these are riddled with precious metals and isotopes, not to mention exotic chemicals. This comet must have been in an orbit that neared my home planet. Robots slowly mine and ingest traces of these materials and when the comet nears our planet again, they will launch and dock with our processing satellites. Or would have, if any satellites were left."

"What's Alice want with 'em?" Jack asked.

"Magnetic oar," she said, followed by a deep thrumming sound.

Porpi was laughing.

The bugs thinned enough to deposit us not far from Alice. They stopped massing and began forming ranks and lines, marching over and around Alice in odd patterns.

"She has found a way to re-knit her lattices in a shorter amount of time. Is this not so, Alice?"

A blue holo-hand appeared, thumbs up.

Two cheers and deep, thrumming later, we sat down and watched the bug dance.

"Porpi?" Jack asked.

"Yes, Jack?"

"What happened to your people?"

She didn't answer for the longest time.

"An asteroid happened."

"It hit your planet?" I said.

"It hit one of our moons. The largest. The shockwave destroyed one side of my world, and the debris destroyed much of the other half. There were only a few hundred thousand of my people left and the atmosphere had become silt."

"Then what?" Jack asked. But I knew the answer.

"You built an ark!"

Porpi had to wait for the translation. Then her eye glittered. "Just so. A bold plan emerged. We had no other planets in reach to find shelter upon, so we decided to wait for ours."

"Huh?"

"Our arks were launched with the entire population and millions of seeds and embryos of fauna and flora, straight toward the black hole that our neighboring star had become."

"You aimed for that black hole? What, on a suicide run?" Jack hollered.

"No, Jack, on a relativistic run," Porpi said.

"You had relatives there?"

Deep thrumming. "Time slows down the faster you go and the deeper gravity is. We intended to use the gravimetric pull of the black hole to increase our speed to near light-speed, intending to veer off just enough to avoid the gravity sink of the black hole. To us, time was constant, but to our planet, thousands of years passed. As we rushed the black hole, our planet was healing, the silt settling, the atmosphere clearing. We hoped to return to a clean world after less than a generation had passed for us."

"But that's not what happened," I said.

She wagged her torso. "Our calculations were flawless in both planetary and relativistic math. What we had not anticipated was that a third math beyond the known two existed. Light speed does not increase smoothly, it leaps geometrically at high gravity. Our calculations broke down the faster we got. We were able to prevent a direct fall into the black hole, but instead of slingshotting out, we spiraled in closer."

"Your people died from math? Figures," Jack said.

"We did not. We knew such a fate was possible, so we had life pods powerful enough to use the hole's gravity against it. My people all escaped; my pod failed."

"So, wait! Your people are okay then? They got out?"

"The pods were powered by the same energy matrix as Alice. They unraveled as hers began to do. They were claimed by the black hole."

"Are you sure? Alice made it out! Maybe your people did too!" I was sure that was it! Whole races couldn't just die, right?

Porpi slumped. "Alice is several thousand revolutions more advanced than our pods. We entered relativistic speed three thousand years ago. To you and Jack, I am

3,228 revolutions old, while to my people, I am little more than an adolescent. And now I am alone."

I had to think about that for a while. Minutes ago, I thought we were going to die out here. Home, Earth, so far away, made me lonely, but even then, I had Jack. Now that Alice was repairing herself quicker, we'd be able to go home, and Earth didn't seem so far. It was there and we would soon be there. Porpi didn't have that. Her planet was probably still there, but no one was home. She was truly alone.

And then it occurred to me that maybe she wasn't.

We'd studied about Mount Saint Helens, the volcano that blew up in America when my parents were little. People had stayed. They knew it was going to blow, and they stayed anyway. Dad had said there were always people like that who stayed in the face of certain doom. Sometimes, he'd said, they survived.

"Porpi!" I called, forgetting that our lifebands kept us in communication despite her standing off by herself. She turned, spearing me with a single black eye.

"Maybe there are people on your planet! You know, people who stayed, like on that volcano!"

Jack squinted at me. "What volcano?"

I waved him off. "It doesn't matter. It's just that someone always stays behind, right? Porpi, I bet someone stayed behind! We can take you back to your world and find them!"

She glided toward us, her great head wagging side-to-side in a universal gesture of "no way."

"No one stayed."

"You don't know that," I said.

"Of course I do."

"You think! You don't know!" I said, parroting my dad's favorite saying.

Her brow scrunched together. "I do know. I can't feel anyone."

"What's that mean?" Jack spouted.

She looked from Jack to me and back to Jack. "You don't feel one another?"

"Only if we touch," I said.

"Touch me and you die," Jack said.

"Touch you and I'd want to die," I said.

Porpi drew back. "I don't understand."

"Makes three of us," Jack said. "What's all this touchy-feely stuff?"

"You cannot sense one another?"

"Not without one of the five senses," I said, confused.

"Only five? Interesting. I thought all people of a kind could sense one another. When my people left our planet, we could feel that no one remained. If they had, they could not survive. When their pods collapsed into the black hole, I felt their translation. When next we enter Para-space, I hope to sense their receiving."

Jack threw his hands into the air and skated off. "I dunno WHAT she's talking about!"

I took a deep breath. "Translating means dying... what does 'receiving' mean?"

She tilted her torso. "Into the presence of the One."

"Is the One... in Para-space?"

"I thought you knew the One. Is this not so? The One is everywhere, but Para-space is thin, where the presence is thick."

"Is that what we feel in there? Why doesn't Jack feel anything?"

"I do not understand Jack," she said.

"No one does," I said.

"And again," my lifeband said in Jack's voice, "I can hear you."

"Sorry, Jack," I said.

He was out of sight beyond a hill of ice, but his voice buzzed on my arm. "It's not like your God and her One is the same thing, Hud, get real. Maybe she's Muslim or something."

"What is Muslim?" Porpi asked.

"Hmmm. They are religious, like me, but their god isn't my God. I don't think, anyway."

"Do they sound different?"

"Who, Muslims?"

"Their god and your god."

"Well, you can't hear God," I said. "Not really, like with your ears or anything."

"Of course not with ears, with -----." Whatever she said didn't translate.

"You can hear God?"

"Of course."

Jack's voice shook from my wrist. "What's he say?"

"Many things."

"Hud, does your God talk to you?"

"Well, sure, you know, through the Bible, and, um, impressions?"

Porpi looked at me.

"Well, see, God loves, you know, his children, and sent Jesus to save them. You know?"

"I do not," Porpi said.

"Oh. Uh, Jesus came to Earth... no, Jesus was God and, I mean, is God, but he died for us, and before that, he had the Jews, only they didn't recognize Him," I said.

Jack popped up beside us. "Smooth, Hud. Real smooth."

"Let me try again. God made everything, right? All the universe, everything," I said.

"The One is the creator. He made all."

"Good, so we're on track, then. Then he made people, and they rebelled."

"Rebelled?"

"Yeah, you know, they didn't obey him."

"Why?" she said.

"Do you know what a snake is?"

"No."

"Um, okay then. They just did. And people were evil and God had to wipe them all out, except for Noah. He had an ark like your people. Then we came back but weren't much better. Then the Jews, his people, got enslaved and released and they wandered, but people were still evil. That's when Jesus came as one of us and preached and stuff. Then he was crucified... uh, killed... and because he was God, he died for us so we could be with him, as his new people, get it?" I blinked down at her.

"The One is love," she said.

"Yeah, like that," I said.

"I don't get it, either," Jack said.

Chapter 12

Whoops!

"I'M HUNGRY, BUT I don't have to pee," Jack said.

That was weird. Me neither. We had been off-Earth for more than a whole day and I can't normally hold it that long.

Porpi was watching the robot miners file off into the mist. She spoke without turning. "The lifebands use waste as fuel."

"I don't think I wanted to know that," Jack said. I had to agree.

She turned. "Alice is ready to leave."

Alice agreed with a blue double-thumbs up.

"What are you going to do, Porpi? Where do you want to go?"

"I have been considering. I can't go home. I don't know any other people who would take me in. Your world sounds... strange..."

"Oh, it is," Jack said. "We're nuts."

"Do your people have relationships with other worlds?"

"Nope," Jack said. "We think we're the only ones."

"Truly?"

I nodded. "Yep."

"Wouldn't that make my presence hard to explain?"

Jack pondered. "Well, it might not go so well."

"We'd have to hide you."

"I have nowhere else to go."

"That's settled, then," I said. "You'll like my folks, though. They'll love to meet you."

"Hud, we can't tell your parents. They'll take away Alice."

"We have to."

"No way. We'll hide her in the cave. Or in my barn."

"Can we argue about this on the way home? My parents are going to kill me!"

"I know," Jack said. "I'll introduce you to my dad. He'll think you're a hallucination. Let's go."

We leaped onto Alice. Porpi stood there.

"Come on," Jack said. "They won't bite and neither will we."

"Scout's honor," I said.

Porpi gingerly climbed aboard.

"Just don't ask about Area 51," Jack said.

Lift-off was smooth, and the comet fell away in rainbow vapor. I would never grow tired of the alien sites out here. In a sudden bout of insight, I was surprised at how quickly I accepted the alien and alien strangeness. Porpi, despite her similarities to a were-dolphin, was still a creature from another star. Yet I've talked with her and taken her as a friend already. Would adults be able to do the same? Would my parents be able to accept my alien friend?

As if reading my thoughts, Porpi asked a stunning question.

"What is a parent?"

Jack scowled. "Is Alice messing up the translation? Parents are moms and dads. Or just dad in my case."

"And these are what?" she said.

"What are what?" I asked.

"Moms and dads."

Jack and I exchanged looks. "You don't have parents?"

Her lip lifted a fraction, showing just the tips of pointed teeth.

"How were you born?" I quickly asked to prevent fully-bared fangs.

She sighed. "Like everyone else."

TO THE MOON, ALICE!

Jack leaned back and tapped his foot. "Well, if it was like us, you'd know what parents are. Explain. Without any yucky details."

Porpi's gaze went from Jack's eyes to mine. "From a Creech. How were you?"

"What's a Creech?" Jack asked.

"Everyone knows what..."

"Aliens!" I said, pointing at Jack and me. I lost track of the comet as it fell away and the sun it had been running from dwindled in the distance.

She sighed again. "The Creech is a vast collection of eggs."

"Who lays the eggs?" I said.

"Lays? I don't understand. The eggs begin as microscopic orbs shed by my people. They mingle and form a Creech. Over several orbits, the eggs mature and a generation comes forth. Is this not how it is on your world?"

"Not exactly."

"Then how?" she said.

OK, Dad and I had had "the talk" last year. There was no way I was going to explain all that. Besides, I wasn't sure if Jack had all the facts. But to my surprise...

"A man and woman," Jack said, "that is a mom and a dad. Make a baby. Just one man, just one lady. A baby. A little person."

"How?"

Jack threw his hands in the air. "It's not like they follow a recipe!"

"Who raises you?" I asked, changing the subject.

"Yeah, you know, who takes care of you when you're a kid? Before you learn stuff," Jack said, disgusted by the whole conversation.

"We are taught in the Creech. We emerge... like this," she said, indicating her person.

"No school?" asked Jack.

"School?"

Jack kicked at the floor with a toe. "I was born on the wrong planet."

"This is the way of every known species. I have never heard of what you describe."

"Well," I conceded, "we didn't explain it very well."

"We're kids," Jack said. "We have to do what adults tell us."

"Your adults told you to fly Alice to different planets?"

"What they don't know doesn't hurt them," Jack said.

Feeling guilty, I turned to see if our Sun was anywhere around, forgetting I wouldn't know it if I saw it. Stars peppered the sky like ice crystals, but none were any larger than another. We were pretty far away from everything.

Blue lights began to flicker across Alice's console.

"Get ready, Jack!" I yelled, and suddenly we were everywhere and nowhere at once.

I tried to pay attention, but quickly got lost in the utter warmth and peace. On just the edge of my hearing, a voice trilled, but I couldn't make out any words. I felt whole and empty all at once. The sensation was timeless... yet seemed longer somehow. I was drawn to everywhere but couldn't reach anything. I wanted to sing but had no voice, to fling myself wide, but had no arms. I felt for Jack, hoping I could sense him and let him know everything was wonderful, but Jack was gone...

And then the moon filled our view and beyond it, Earth!

I looked around and saw tears streaming from giant black eyes, a look of pure joy on Porpi's face.

Jack was curled up on the floor of Alice. He whimpered. When I crouched to grab his shoulder, he didn't move. I peered up at Porpi.

"They have arrived!" Then concern, "What is wrong with Jack?"

"Who's arrived? I said, glancing around in a panic.

"My people. They have been taken into the presence, to the final home."

"That's good," I said absently. Wait. "All of them?" Concern for Jack gave way to Sunday School teaching on Heaven and Hell.

"Of course," she said.

"Is anyone ever not 'arrived'?" I asked.

"Of course not!" she said, horrified.

"I think that's what's happening to Jack. I think he's being... rejected!"

Jack gagged on the floor as Alice swung around the moon, revealing Earth in all its glory.

Porpi's mouth fell open.

So did mine.

On all our other trips, we approached Earth from the dayside, the continents brown and green under white clouds and surrounded by shining blue water.

This was the night side. The continents blazed with fire, artificial light shining up to the heavens, the clouds not thick enough to block it. Even the oceans had scattered lights. Islands or something, maybe.

Jack struggled to his feet.

Alice fell toward the great planet as Jack wretched. Fortunately, our stomachs were empty.

"What are the darker spots? Forests?" Porpi asked.

"Water," Jack croaked.

"I'm sorry, Jack," she said, "I have none."

"No, the dark spots, that's water. Oceans."

Porpi's eyes grew larger still, her face pulling back into tight shock.

"Water? On the surface? How is that possible?"

"Your planet doesn't have oceans or lakes?" I said.

"No planet does!"

"Ta-da!" Jack said, raising his hand to the world.

Porpi gaped.

Off our bow, an odd-looking satellite came spinning into view.

"Alice, can that see us?" I shouted.

A blue thumbs up.

"Get us out of here! We can't be seen!"

Alice sprinted the other way, then jigged as another satellite jumped into sight. And another. Alice spiraled through dozens of space machines, making our empty stomachs lurch. Jack squealed while I clamped down hard and moaned through clenched teeth.

We entered atmosphere and stopped abruptly in a heavy cloud bank. The mist swirled around the force field as we caught our breath.

"Who knew we had that many satellites?" Jack said.

"Alice, can you get us home without being caught on camera?" I asked.

One thumbs-up, one down.

"It's really late, isn't it?" I said.

Two thumbs up.

"Jack," I said... knowing my continued good health meant getting home as soon as possible. Jack seemed to read my mind.

"OK, Alice," he said. "Drop into Hud's backyard and, as soon as he jumps off, speed me and Porpi to my barn, got it?"

No thumbs up or down, just a stomach-dropping plummet to Earth. I squeezed my eyes shut as the ground rushed up.

Next thing I knew, Jack shoved me, and I rolled onto the grass. Jack yelled something, but Alice was already too far away for me to hear it, my lifeband trapped between my body and the ground. I jumped up, stomach growling, steeled myself for parental fury, and launched myself at the back doors. The knob stuck at first, refusing to turn in my grip, but then it glowed briefly—a spark from my force field?—and it turned, the door yielding as I pushed through.

Lights splashed the interior, and I realized... this wasn't my house!

"Cornelius, who the heck is that?"

I spun and a girl... no, a woman... was looking at me. She held a plate with a half-eaten slice of cake and in her other hand, a fork turned over and held as a weapon. I put my hands up.

"Sorry! Wrong house!" I shouted.

"Don't move," she said. "Cornelius, why'd you let this kid in?"

"He is your brother, Ela," came a voice from everywhere. A wall suddenly erupted with a 3-D image of me!

The cake hit the ground.

"Hudson?" she said.

———◈———

To be continued...

Rejoin Hud, Jack, and Porpi in the next volume, **Officers and Aliens.**

They've returned to a world they barely recognize, with people they'd known but now don't. America has been forever changed in geology and technology. Old friends are now old friends, and, oh yeah, there's an alien on Earth that the government wants at all costs...